Liz hung up the phone and faced her husband

"So! That was your lover," Francisco said, his cold eyes regarding her flushed features contemptuously.

"John is not my lover!" Liz exclaimed, her eyes beginning to flash angrily.

"Then perhaps I should call him your fiancé? Although I find it a little difficult to imagine anyone having a fiancé and a husband at one time."

"I don't really care what you call him, Francisco, provided you understand that I have no intention of withdrawing the divorce suit," said Liz, raising her chin defiantly as he grasped her arm and growled her name. "And as for your settlement," she spat, angrily shaking off his hand, "I wouldn't accept a penny of your money if I were starving on the street!"

WELCOME
TO THE WONDERFUL WORLD
OF *Harlequin Romances*

Interesting, informative and entertaining,
each Harlequin Romance portrays an appealing
and original love story. With a varied array
of settings, we may lure you on an African safari,
to a quaint Welsh village, or an exotic Riviera
location—anywhere and everywhere that adventurous
men and women fall in love.

As publishers of Harlequin Romances, we're
extremely proud of our books. Since 1949,
Harlequin Enterprises has built its publishing
reputation on the solid base of quality and
originality. Our stories are the most popular
paperback romances sold in North America; every
month, six new titles are released and sold at
nearly every book-selling store in Canada and the
United States.

A free catalogue listing all Harlequin Romances
can be yours by writing to the

HARLEQUIN READER SERVICE,
(In the U.S.) 1440 South Priest Drive, Tempe, AZ 85281
(In Canada) Stratford, Ontario N5A 6W2

We sincerely hope you enjoy reading
this Harlequin Romance.

Yours truly,

THE PUBLISHERS
  Harlequin Romances

Passionate Enemies

by

KATHRYN CRANMER

Harlequin Books

TORONTO • NEW YORK • LOS ANGELES • LONDON
AMSTERDAM • PARIS • SYDNEY • HAMBURG
STOCKHOLM • ATHENS • TOKYO • MILAN

Original hardcover edition published in 1982
by Mills & Boon Limited

ISBN 0-373-02517-3

Harlequin Romance first edition December 1982

CHAPTER ONE

THE rain lashed down wildly, whipping the wet leaves in gusts across the road, and Liz hurried along the path, profoundly grateful for the warmth and protection of her fur-lined raincoat and knee-length boots. She was forced to concede the fact that there were some compensations in having a wealthy husband, although there were many problems too. She shivered and pulled the hood closer to her face . . . more problems than most people realised; life was not all champagne dinners and holidays in the sun.

Screwing up her eyes against the driving rain, she peered ahead to where the luxury block of flats overlooked the comparative peace of Regent's Park. She would be soaked before reaching the flat. How foolish she had been to venture out in this weather when she could just as easily have left her letter with the commissionaire to post later.

She sighed bitterly. The truth of the matter was that the flat felt like a lonely prison without Francisco's presence, and she had just had to get away, if only for a few minutes. Gasping with relief, she gained the foyer of the exclusive building, taking down her hood and shaking the rain from her clothing vigorously, quite unaware of the charming picture that she made, her ash blonde hair tumbling in silky profusion from the confines of her hood, raindrops glistening on the ends of her startlingly dark eyelashes.

In fact Liz was totally without conceit in so far as her appearance was concerned. Her figure was good, it was true, her waist narrow and her breasts and hips slim but feminine, but she was still unable to see how she had attracted someone as exciting as Francisco to her. She had always regretted her rather long, aquiline nose and envied

5

her friends their retroussé models, unaware that when accompanied by a generous, full-lipped mouth it gave her an intriguing air of hauteur, yet with an underlying promise of sensual warmth which many men found completely fascinating.

'Shocking day, Mrs Ramirez!' The commissionaire's friendly voice interrupted the trend of her thoughts.

'Mm, I don't think I'll risk going out again today,' she agreed with a smile.

'Going to hang on here for another ten minutes or so myself, see if it improves. Bill's on duty now,' he added, indicating the uniformed figure in the small reception room.

'Well, I hope the weather clears for you, Mr Dodds. See you later,' she added, stepping into the lift and pressing the button for the top floor.

'That's a real pleasant young woman,' Jack Dodds remarked, indicating Liz's departing figure. 'Always got a friendly word, never too proud to pass the time of day with a chap. Not like some of these people,' he added in denigrating tones, 'only speak to you if they want something doing and then they give you a tip without looking at you. 'Fraid you might give 'em the evil eye, I shouldn't wonder.'

'What about that husband of 'ers—foreigner, isn't 'e? Arrogant sort of chap, lot older than his wife, I should think,' commented Bill, pausing for a moment in the process of rolling a very professional-looking cigarette.

'Spanish, he is, one of your aristocrats I reckon, not friendly like his lady, but he's always very polite—a real gentleman he is, not like some,' Jack reiterated with a wry grimace. 'He's in Spain on business at the moment, so Mrs Ramirez tells me.'

'Funny thing 'im leaving 'er here on her own,' Bill interposed, drawing thoughtfully on his cigarette. 'They've not been married long either, have they, Jack?'

'No! Still, it takes all sorts to make a world.' Jack Dodds stated philsophically. 'I'm going to make a dash for it now, Bill,' he added, peering hopefully at a temporary break in the clouds. 'See you tomorrow, mate.'

Liz entered the familiar luxury of the top floor flat and shed her dripping raincoat and boots with relief. In tight brown cord trousers and a slim-fitting cream silk shirt she appeared barely old enough to be a bride of more than six months. After running a careless brush through her tangled hair she walked rather dejectedly towards the streamlined kitchen. In truth the very thought of food was totally nauseating. However, as she had eaten nothing but a bowl of cereal since getting up in the morning she knew she would have to make the effort to digest something.

A search through the fridge revealed some firm tomatoes and a slab of cheese that Mrs Hammond, the daily woman, must have bought that morning. Liz extracted them unenthusiastically and slowly began to butter the bread for a sandwich, deciding on a glass of apple juice as an accompaniment.

As she chewed desultorily on her sandwich she tried once more to decide just how and where her relationship with Francisco had begun to weaken. Ten months ago their love had been so strong it had seemed as though they could overcome any obstacle. Their first few meetings at the home of a wealthy school friend had seemed like an unbelievable dream come true. Prince Charming and Cinderella, Liz thought with a wry grin, for that had been other people's assessment of the situation as well as her own, she knew. That Francisco Ramirez, eldest son of one of Spain's most wealthy and powerful families, should fall in love with her, the daughter of an invalid ex-miner, had seemed impossible.

Picking up her crockery and half-eaten sandwich, Liz moved wearily towards the sink. Disposing of the sandwich with a shudder of distaste, she washed the dishes carefully and left them to drain in the rack. Pushing open the door to the elegantly understated sitting room, she went to sit dejectedly on the cream leather couch, her thoughts turning once more to the early days of their relationship. She sighed wearily. With the benefit of hindsight it was clear to see that the passion which had flared between them had made barriers of class and culture appear surmountable, but Liz knew the time had come to stop pretending; she had ignored the facts for too long, but they had to be faced. Passion had precipitated the marriage and now, all too obviously, Francisco was regretting the fact.

Lethargically Liz swung her feet to the ground and moved with unconscious grace towards the expensive stereo unit, extracting a record from the cupboard below the deck. Perhaps some music would help to alter the totally futile direction of her thoughts. As the disruptive chords of one of Beethoven's final quartets filled the room, images of her wedding day almost imperceptibly intruded.

Much of the day was an unreal haze in her memory, almost as though someone else had taken her place for the occasion. Yet she still remembered clearly every detail of the beautiful bouquet of white rosebuds she had carried, and the cool strength of Francisco's hand as it held hers after the ceremony. The wedding night, too, was still a warm and living memory. Francisco was a skilled and passionate lover, and he had broken down the barriers of her inexperience with ease and consummate skill.

Impatiently she rose to her feet, thrusting the disturbing thoughts away, turning off the stereo and stopping the tortured brilliance of the music in midstream. She realised now, of course, that it was after she started her first term at university that the cracks began to appear in her marriage. It was not as though she had begun to go out to discos or bars. She never enjoyed going out without Francisco and had rarely gone anywhere except to lectures, and Francisco had often collected her from these.

It was ironic really that their first major row had been

precipitated by Steve Farren, a language student, newly engaged to Pam Ellis, the closest friend that Liz had made at college. Francisco had called to collect her and had seen Steve put his arm casually across her shoulders in a perfectly innocent gesture. He had seen the incident in the worst possible light and had refused to listen to anything that she had to say in her own defence. Liz shivered inwardly even now as she remembered the look of uncontrollable fury on his distorted features.

Their quarrel had finally been resolved when he had held her in his arms and made love to her. There was no doubt that his lovemaking had been just as passionate as ever, but Liz had felt a new quality in his passion after that day. It was almost as though Francisco hated her and sought to give vent to his feelings in the violence of his lovemaking.

There had been a gradual deterioration in their relationship since then. Francisco's manner towards her had become painfully polite, only in bed did he seem unable to maintain his aura of cool hauteur. Moodily she went to stare out of the penthouse window, completely oblivious to the magnificent panorama before her, the rain-washed buildings glistening and steaming now, in the light of the newly emerging sun.

She had placed all her hopes on his realising that he still needed her and loved her during the separation of his visit to Spain, although she realised that the fact that she had not accompanied him would be another black mark against her so far as his family were concerned. She sighed, leaning her forehead against the cool glass in a curiously weary gesture. It was a false hope anyway, she was beginning to realise. One telephone call to say that he had arrived safely and then only one brief, cold note to say that his return had been delayed, were hardly conducive to a passionate reconciliation.

The ringing of the telephone galvanised her into action forcing her out of her lethargy for the moment. Perhaps it will be Francisco! Dear God, let it be Francisco. I'll promise anything if only he'll come home quickly, she begged almost unconsciously as she hurried into the hall and lifted the receiver.

'Hello, hello, Francisco, is that you—are you O.K.?'

'Liz, it's Andrew—from university. I take it that your jailer isn't at home at the moment if you expected to hear from him, eh? That means we can talk in peace, I guess.'

'Oh, Andrew,' Liz said heavily, trying to disguise her depression at the identity of her caller. After all, it was not Andrew's fault that Francisco could not be bothered to telephone her.

'Do I sense a certain lack of enthusiasm in your voice, my love? I'm not boasting when I say that at least half the unmarried females in London are waiting to lay their hearts at my feet, and all I get from you is oh, Andrew!'

'Oh, Andrew!' Liz said again, laughing in spite of herself.

'There you go again—a definite lack of enthusiasm. What you need, my girl, is a night out on the tiles, without your Spanish bodyguard.'

'It wouldn't be fair to go out without Francisco, you know that, Andrew. He would misunderstand completely. . . .'

'What! You mean to say that he really doesn't lock you in the house every evening when you get home? That really is only a rumour?'

'Be serious for a moment, Andrew, will you? It's only reasonable to expect a wife to be with her husband, you must admit. If you were married you wouldn't expect your wife to go out in the evenings without you—I know that.'

'If I had the good fortune to be married to as beautiful and charming a wife as that—that—creep, I'd treat her with a damned sight more consideration than he treats you!'

'Don't, Andrew! Please,' Liz murmured, trying to still

the sudden rush of tears that threatened to overwhelm her. 'I love Francisco, you know that, and you have no right to say those things.' To her shame the tears which had been threatening to fall all day were now uncontrollable. 'I must go now, there's someone at the door,' she managed to say, before dropping the receiver and subsiding on to the floor, finally giving way to her grief.

As she washed her face half an hour later she was forced to admit that to give way to her feelings for once had been a blessed relief. Her mood of utter dejection had lifted slightly, although she wished her self-control had not broken in Andrew's hearing. It was likely now that all her friends at university would hear how upset she had been. It had always been possible in the past to hide her distress, and pretend that she did not mind Francisco's overly possessive attitude.

Of course, no one knew of his increasing coldness towards her, for which even the continuing passion of his lovemaking could not compensate. Oh God! Why did her thoughts always keep returning to the times when Francisco held her in his arms and she could feel the hard strength of his body next to hers, mastering her with his passion? It felt so right to give herself totally to him, to allow him to dominate her. Why could she not just bow to his will all the time—give up her studies as he really wished her to do, and wave goodbye to any vestige of independence? What good was her stupid pride when it made her so unhappy?

Liz moved slowly around the kitchen, knowing that soon she would have to force herself to eat yet another meal, when the food tasted like sawdust and made her want to be ill. Already she was beginning to lose weight, and her too slender face with its pallor and heavy eyes would soon cease to attract Francisco. Once the slender thread of physical attraction snapped she knew that she would no longer have any hold over him.

The doorbell began to ring urgently and she was

unable to prevent the feverish sense of anticipation, which she knew to be quite unfounded. If Francisco was coming home he would surely have let her know. Anyway, he was expecting to be another week in Spain, and if he found the company more congenial there—as he no doubt would—he might stay even longer, she reflected bitterly.

Despite these sensible thoughts Liz found that her hands were trembling as she struggled to unlock the door and slide the bolt, and she knew that her face was ridiculously expectant as she opened the door.

'Hello, Liz.' It was Andrew Mellor's worried face that confronted her. Surely she ought to be inured to disappointment by this time, and yet her heart plummeted sickeningly as she realised it was not Francisco.

'Hey, steady on, love!' Andrew's strong arms were around her shoulders and then somehow she was sitting on the couch in the living room as he poured her a large measure of brandy.

'Oh, I can't drink that stuff, Andrew! Honestly I don't need it—I'm perfectly O.K., really I am.'

'Look, you can't see the colour of your face—I can. Do as you're told and drink this up like a good girl!'

'Well, thanks for the compliment,' Liz said wryly, drinking the fiery liquid and gasping as the heat took her breath away. Andrew was right, it did do one good, she thought, as the golden warmth began to invade her cold limbs.

'You know perfectly well that however pale you are you knock every other woman within a ten-mile radius for a six!' He paused a moment, sliding his arm determinedly around Liz's shoulders. 'You're beautiful, adorable—surely you know that?'

Perhaps it was the relaxing effect of the brandy, or maybe the result of her desperate need for reassurance and comfort, but she made no attempt to pull away from him, only turning her face into his hard-muscled shoulder—imagining for a moment that it was Francisco holding her and comforting her. . . . Even when Andrew's lips began to move caressingly in her hair there were no warning bells. She was lost in her thoughts of Francisco and it was only his lips that she felt.

She was brought sharply back to reality when his lips descended on to her own, urgently attempting to force her to respond to him. But no matter how passionately he made love to her she could no longer pretend that this was Francisco. There was no languorous sweetness invading her limbs, only an urgent desire to escape, and her own hands moved frantically to push him away from her. She began to struggle desperately in his arms—then opened her eyes directly into Francisco's shocked and accusing stare.

'*Dios!* Lizbeth! Never would I have believed it!'

'Francisco, Francisco, it isn't what you think! Please believe me!' Liz's anguished cry brought Andrew to his senses. His eyes still glazed with passion, he rose unsteadily to his feet to face Francisco, certain now that Liz returned his love and that her withdrawal had only occurred after she had seen Francisco in the doorway.

'So the Spanish jailer has returned! A pity you didn't leave it a few minutes later, then you really would have seen something to rage about.' Andrew's air of bravado and provocative words were all that was needed to turn Francisco's shock and horror into ungovernable rage. With an unmentionable oath he launched himself across the space that separated them, knocking the younger man backwards on to a chair with tremendous force. Liz knew that she had to stop the fight somehow. Francisco's earlier anger had been mild compared with his present rage, and Andrew looked almost equally incensed, as he struggled out of the chair wiping the blood from his mouth with the back of his hand.

Liz was afraid that if the fight continued one or both of the men would be seriously hurt. Either way Francisco would suffer. Liz found that even now—even when she knew that their marriage might be irrevocably over—she could not bear to think of him being injured, and she knew that if news of the brawl, and the reason for it, leaked to the press, his pride would suffer a severe blow. A Spaniard's masculine pride was very important to him, and Francisco's must already have taken a beating, coming home and finding his wife in the arms of another man—however innocent it might have been on her part.

'Stop! Stop this minute, both of you!' Her voice broke ignominiously as she saw that her protests were being ignored. The two men continued to struggle and Liz knew she must take more decisive action. Hurriedly she ran into the kitchen to fill a bowl with water, memories of her mother stopping quarrelling dogs with a well aimed bucket full of water springing to her mind. If it worked for dogs there was always the chance that it would stop the two men.

Only a few moments had passed since she left the room, yet already a swelling bruise disfigured Andrew's cheek-bone, and she noted it without surprise. Francisco's anger had not abated, and she sensed that he had the upper hand in this fight. His slim body was deceptive, of course. He was like a hunting animal—fined down to the essentials, lean-muscled and brutally strong when he chose to exert himself.

Liz took the scene in at a glance and without stopping to consider further, threw the water with tremendous force. It landed squarely over Francisco, leaving Andrew almost totally dry. Francisco stopped short in the act of delivering yet another damaging punch to his opponent's face. His look of surprise would have been amusing in other circumstances, Liz thought, preventing herself from laughing hysterically, with difficulty. As Francisco realised what had happened his face darkened again with anger, and the hysterical laughter died in her throat.

'You wanton little bitch! You would do anything to protect your lover, would you not? *Dios!* It would give me great pleasure to shake the breath out of you!' As he spoke he advanced threateningly towards Liz.

Thoughts of self-preservation were uppermost in her distraught mind, but deep down she knew instinctively that Francisco would never hurt her physically. More painful than any blow however was the look of hatred that blazed in his eyes, destroying all hope that he might believe her version of the story. Unable to utter a word in her own defence, she fought to quell the feelings of despair that threatened to engulf her.

'My God, you really are a son of a bitch, Ramirez, aren't you?' Andrew's words penetrated her dulled senses and she became aware that Francisco's grasp had slackened, as he turned his attention back to Andrew.

'Andrew, please! Just leave us! Go—go now, for my sake, please!' She found that she was unable to raise her voice above a whisper, but both men turned towards her, a cruel sneer on Francisco's face as he said:

'Yes, go, Mellor! I have finished with you—for the moment. Be thankful that we are not in my own country where the arm of my family is long!' He turned almost contemptuously away from the younger man, his hard eyes coming to rest once more on Liz's strained and pallid features. 'So! Now I can give all my attention to you my so lovely wife, hm? I seem to remember that you have enjoyed my attentions in the past, *cara*! Is that not so?' His words were spoken in a voice full of bitter mockery, and Liz was unable to resist attempting to protest her innocence once more.

'Please, Francisco, listen to me! I didn't encourage Andrew, truly I didn't—you must believe me!' Her voice faltered as he gave a sneering laugh.

'No, *cara*, you were positively discouraging him when you heard me come through the door. This I know! Did I not see your struggles for myself?' He laughed again, mockingly, one hand tracing the delicate outline of her face with studied insolence. 'However, fortunately for me,

I was not—how do you say—born yesterday. I am aware that you would not have been struggling if I had not come in during that charming scene. How unfortunate for you, my dear, that I felt the need of your so attractive company and finished my business quickly to give you a—er—pleasant surprise.'

His drawling words were interrupted by Andrew's angry but triumphant tones. 'Well, I'm damned glad you did come in at that time. Liz would never admit what a son of a bitch you were, but by heavens, I should think she knows now!'

'Andrew, please!' Liz realised that she had forgotten Andrew's presence, but it was obvious that she must get him out of the flat immediately, before Francisco's frail hold on his temper broke once again.

'You must go! Now, please!' Liz turned pleading eyes towards him and he stepped involuntarily towards her.

'Spare me this tender scene!' Francisco said harshly. 'You will have to wait your turn to enjoy my wife's company, Mellor. Now, get out of my house! You are trespassing, and be thankful that I am a civilised man. My forebears would not have dealt with you so kindly. Now go,' he threatened angrily, 'before I change my mind!'

'Come with me, Liz,' said Andrew insistently as he moved towards her, his face white and rather desperate. Liz felt a flood of affection for him; he really did care for her and it was not his fault that things had happened as they had.

'No, Andrew, I can't. Please go now! I'll be fine, you'll see. Go, quickly!' she begged, conscious of her husband's cold eyes regarding her and wondering whether, in fact, she would be safe in the presence of this hard-faced stranger. She moved towards Andrew and urged him out of the door, promising to call him if she had need of him, as he protested bitterly at her wish to stay in the flat with Francisco.

'He is my husband, Andrew,' she said quietly. 'And he

has good reason for feeling angry, wouldn't you say?' she added, turning her pale, sad face to his.

He grasped her hands firmly, raising them to his lips as she attempted to pull away. 'Don't worry, love, everything will be fine. We'll get married as soon as you can get a divorce from that—devil! I can leave university and get a job in Dad's business. It's what he wants me to do anyway, but I wish you'd come with me now. I don't want to leave you here with him,' he added, with a hard glance in Francisco's direction.

He seemed unaware that these plans for her future had distressed Liz rather than reassured her, and she felt too upset to do more than urge him to leave as quickly as possible. Explanations would have to come later.

'You must go! We can't talk now. Later—things will be different later,' she added rather wildly, only anxious to return to the room and attempt to explain to Francisco, unaware that Andrew would see her words as acquiescing in his plans for the future.

She returned to the room, expecting to be met by an angry tirade, only to find it empty. She stopped, her hands going involuntarily to her face, a feeling of numbed horror washing over her at the thought that Francisco had already left the flat, to be closely followed by one of heartfelt relief. How could she be such a fool? She had been standing in the doorway and he hadn't gone past her. Purposefully she headed for the door of their bedroom. No good would come of postponing their next meeting; she must try to convince him. She must! If he truly loved her he would come to accept her explanation . . . he just had to!

Stifling any doubts as to the rightness of her actions, she thrust open the bedroom door, only to come to an embarrassed halt at the sight which met her eyes. Francisco was dressed only in a pair of brief shorts and was in the process of pulling a clean shirt over his heavily muscled shoulders. Even in her present distressed condition, the sight of his lean tanned body did not fail to move her, and almost unconsciously a warm flush of colour rose in her cheeks.

'Oh! I'm sorry, Francisco! I never thought——' she stammered incoherently, dragging her eyes away from his disturbing presence with a deliberate effort.

'Stay! I wish to speak with you!' Francisco's words were a command, but still she continued to retreat.

'I'll wait in the living room, for... for... when you're dressed.'

The laughter which greeted these words grated harshly in her ears.

'Oh, come, come, my dear! Is it not a little late for this maidenly modesty? I am sure the male body can hold no secrets from you—a new lover and a new husband all in the space of six months—this display of virtue is a little late, wouldn't you say?' he added mockingly, moving towards her and making no attempt to continue dressing.

One long arm reached out lazily and pulled her into the room, slamming the door firmly behind her. Liz retreated hastily from the expression in his eyes, until she was leaning weakly against the wall, trying to still the trembling in her limbs, which she knew was as much a response to the overwhelming physical attraction of the man as of her fear of his anger.

Indolently he rested his hands at either side of her head, staring mockingly into her pleading eyes.

'You are wanton, my Lizbeth! I have long suspected it—now I am certain! You have played me for a fool, is that not so? And I, poor, weak idiot that I am, have been too enamoured to see clearly. But no longer, eh? I owe your ... friend Mellor my thanks. He has caused me to see you in your true light, my love! A beautiful but un-scrupulous woman.' As he spoke his hand moved from the wall to caress her face and neck, lingering in the open neckline of her shirt, even now making her tremble with longing for him and yet feeling bitterly ashamed at the

betrayal of her own body of which she was sure he was
fully aware.

The sight of her soft, trembling mouth and the yielding
softness of her skin beneath his caressing hands appeared
to be his undoing. With a groan, part anger, part passion,
he tightened his arms around her and his mouth descended with urgent insistence on to her own, forcing her
lips apart to receive his kiss. Her own response to his passion was instinctive and even had she wished to defy him
she knew that her body would have refused to obey her.

Languorous sweetness invaded her being as he urgently
unfastened the buttons of her shirt, dwelling for a moment
on the soft warmth of her midriff before undoing the fastening of her bra and caressing her naked breasts with
increasing urgency, lowering his lips to their soft fullness,
making her tremble with the overwhelming emotions that
he aroused by his actions. When he abruptly released her,
her hands moved involuntarily to pull his mouth back to
hers.

'Ah, do not worry, Lizbeth. I do not mean to deprive
you of my attentions.'

Through the passion Liz heard unmistakable contempt
in his voice, whether for himself or for her she could not
tell, but she knew that his opinion of her had not altered,
except perhaps for the worse.

'Your lover did not manage to satisfy you on this occasion, eh? Well, do not worry, little one! I mean to satisfy
you, you will not be able to complain about my lack of
attention, *querida*.' These words were uttered in a grating
contemptuous voice that made a mockery of the tender
words of love that he murmured as his lips claimed hers
again. Belatedly she began to struggle as he lifted her in
his arms and carried her towards the bed, but he seemed
impervious to her fists beating against his naked chest and
as his kisses became more demanding, her struggles turned
to acquiescence and her fingers moved caressingly against
the dark hairs of his chest. As he removed the last of her

clothing Liz gave herself totally to him, without thought for the future, conscious only of his demanding nearness, of the hard strength of his body and the yielding weakness of her own.

She awoke in the darkness feeling drowsily content, but as memory returned she turned urgently in the bed, expecting Francisco's pillow to be empty, now that he had demonstrated his overwhelming power over her. She stared straight into the mocking gaze of her husband.

'So—you look surprised, Lizbeth. Were you perhaps dreaming of your English lover and expecting to find him here? I am sorry to disappoint you,' he added harshly, 'but I intend to make this a night to remember, Lizbeth. When you are with your youthful friend you will think of me and of this night together.'

'Please, Francisco! I don't want to be with Andrew. It wasn't as you think,' she added tremulously. 'Just love me, please! Please, Francisco, love me!'

'That is exactly what I intend to do,' he muttered with a groan, drawing her roughly into his arms and devouring her mouth with his own. . . .

Liz finally slept as dawn broke, a faint hope for the future growing in her breast. Surely after the night's passionate lovemaking Francisco could not intend to leave her. It was obvious that he was still deeply attracted to her—there was hope, surely there was hope. She would give up her studies and devote herself entirely to him; surely that would satisfy him? With this comforting thought she drifted again into unconsciousness.

In the cold light of day things did not look so promising. She awoke to find herself alone in the large bed, an indentation in the pillow the only sign of Francisco's occupation. She must just hope for the best; after last night surely he must still care for her a little. As her memory of the night returned the hot colour burned in her cheeks. She had responded to his lovemaking shamelessly. The last core of her reserve had melted as he plundered her body and his violent passion had achieved her total surrender. She knew that her love for him put her in his power.... Angrily she thrust this thought to the back of her mind. She must hurry and dress and discover what Francisco intended to do.

She slid her legs out of bed and stretched languorously, her hair tumbling in silky profusion around her shoulders. Catching sight of her reflection in the dressing table mirror, she moved tentatively towards it. She felt as though last night must have made its mark on her, but apart from the swollen fullness of her lips, she seemed completely untouched by Francisco's devastating invasion of her body.

'So! You are admiring your beauty, Lizbeth! And why should you not indeed? You are beautiful—a beautiful, cheating wanton! A trap for a foolish man, is that not so?'

Liz shivered involuntarily at the expression in Francisco's eyes. Gone was the glowing passion of the night; they were as cold and hard as pebbles.

'Francisco, please!' she murmured pleadingly, moving uncertainly towards him. 'Don't be like this, please!'

'Ah no, Lizbeth,' he said brutally, retreating slightly, as though to escape the appeal of her tremulous lips and naked body. 'The time for love is past, *querida*! Your appeals will not move me,' he added harshly. 'I am no longer blind, now I see you as you are. A loose woman who saw the chance to marry a wealthy man, and took it! Who would have believed that I could have been taken in twice by the same trick?' he added with a derisive shake of his head.

'Please . . . I don't understand?'

'No, you do not understand, do you, Lizbeth?' Francisco replied, running his hands through his still damp hair in a curiously weary gesture. 'I kept the story of my past love to myself. Poor fool that I was, I did not wish to upset you.

'I met Helen at Oxford,' he continued in self-derisory

tones. 'She was beautiful, Oh, not like you . . . no, nothing like you, Lizbeth,' he added, his glance flicking over her in cold appraisal. 'She was dark, almost Spanish in appearance. Both her parents were doctors in Oxford and we met at a college dance. She was surrounded by admiring males and I was young enough to be flattered when she chose to spend her time with me. We fell in love. At least I fell in love, and she . . . she seemed as deeply in love as I.

'I had a good friend, Bill Evans, with whom I shared a flat,' he continued unemotionally, moving to stare with unseeing eyes out of the penthouse window. 'We were all good friends together and although I sensed that Bill desired her, truth to tell it made my possession more sweet.

'One day I returned to the flat unexpectedly. I had a headache, I believe . . . something and nothing,' he said with a dismissive gesture. 'I must have entered very silently, or perhaps they were too engrossed in their conversation to hear me.' He shrugged at the memory and continued slowly, 'It was a moment or two before I realised that I was not alone in the flat. I was going to shout a greeting, but then I recognised her voice coming from his bedroom, and I listened unashamedly outside the door.

'To cut a long story short, it appeared that they had been lovers for some time. Bill was naturally anxious for her to break off her relationship with me. It is never pleasant when you are in love to think that someone else shares the object of your desires,' Francisco said with a contemptuous glance at Liz's frozen figure. 'Helen was not so anxious to bring our . . . friendship to an end. Bill was not well endowed financially and it seemed that Helen's aim in life was to snare a wealthy husband. Apparently she had me marked out as the ideal candidate.'

'But why did Bill not warn you?' asked Liz, the words

tumbling out of their own volition. If only you'd told me earlier, she wanted to scream at him . . . if only I'd known the truth, your jealousy and distrust wouldn't have seemed so unreasonable, perhaps I would have responded differently. The words clamoured in her brain, but Francisco turned his cold gaze upon her and they were never spoken.

'Ah yes . . . Bill,' he continued slowly. 'He loved Helen, or thought he did, and she would no doubt have refused to share her favours with him had he warned me of her duplicity. To do him justice I think perhaps he would have warned me in the end,' he shrugged dismissively. 'In the event it was not necessary and within a few months I had put her out of my mind . . . apart from thanking God for a narrow escape from a scheming bitch. I swore that I would never be fooled by a woman again. You did well, Lizbeth, you broke down the barriers which I had erected around myself, in a remarkably short time. Perhaps you missed your vocation, my so beautiful wife. Your acting had me completely fooled.'

'I swear that I wasn't acting, Francisco. Please believe me!' Liz pleaded in anguished tones. 'I love you—you must believe me!'

He cast her a glance full of contempt and continued as though there had been no interruption, 'Oh, you need not worry! I shall see that you are well provided for. You will still be able to live in the manner to which you have become accustomed. Now, get dressed and then come into the living room—we have things to discuss before I leave,' he added harshly, his eyes travelling over her body in contemptuous appraisal, before he turned abruptly and walked out of the room.

After Francisco had left the flat Liz sat listlessly in the living room, unable to accept that his departure was a permanent thing. When the doorbell finally rang she ran to answer it, in the forlorn hope that he had changed his mind—that he had come back to her—instead she was confronted by a very worried-looking Andrew Mellor.

'My God, Liz, are you all right? Has he hurt you, darling? You look dreadful! I knew I should never have left you,' he added, grasping her hands and drawing her further into the hall, closing the door with a careless hand. 'If he's touched you I swear I'll make him suffer,' he muttered grimly, taking in her pale and tear-stained cheeks and the rather desperate expression in her eyes.

With an effort Liz pulled out of his grasp and walked into the room.

'He hasn't beaten me or anything, Andrew, you don't need to worry,' she said wearily, sinking on to the sofa, pushing the hair away from her eyes with a careless gesture.

'He must have done something pretty dreadful, Liz. I'm not a fool, you know,' he added quietly, sinking beside her on to the sofa and taking her hands tenderly between his own.

'Oh yes! Yes, he's done something dreadful,' Liz answered in a grief-stricken voice, and to her horror the tears which had refused to bring relief earlier began to course silently down her cheeks.

'What is it, darling? What is it?' he urged insistently.

'He's left me, Andrew! He's left me and he won't be coming back! I shall never see him again,' she added, burying her face in her hands.

Immediately his arms went around her, drawing her head on to his chest and rocking her gently in his arms.

'Is that all?' he said softly, relief evident in his voice. 'Don't worry, honey, I meant what I said yesterday. I'm not going to leave you. We'll get married as soon as you can get a divorce and until then I'll look after you. Don't cry, Liz,' he urged insistently.

'Andy, you don't understand,' Liz said desperately, moving out of the protective circle of his arms. 'It's not so straightforward. I love Francisco—I love him desperately,' she added, as he would have interrupted her. She reached out and touched his hand gently as she saw the bewilderment on his face. 'I know you thought I struggled when you kissed me because I saw Francisco. That's what he thinks too, but it's not so. I didn't hear him—I just didn't want you to kiss me,' she explained gently.

'Well, you gave a damned good imitation of enjoying my attention earlier,' Andrew said bitterly, recoiling a little from the pity which he saw on Liz's face.

'I know, Andrew, and I'm sorry—truly I am. I don't want to hurt you, but I must tell you the truth. I was hurt and angry that Francisco hadn't contacted me while he was away. Your kindness was a sort of . . . salve, I guess.' She shrugged helplessly. 'I never intended it to go so far—it was my fault. I know you would never have tried to kiss me if I hadn't seemed to want it.'

'I see! So you don't care for me! It was all a put-up job,' he added, his eyes flashing angrily. 'My God, you had me fooled! I really thought you loved me! But it's still that Spanish husband of yours you're hankering for. It's bloody ironic,' he added, laughing bitterly and rising to his feet to pace angrily around the room.

'I'm crazy about you, but you aren't interested. All you want is that son of a bitch of a husband of yours, and you don't exist as far as he's concerned,' he continued cruelly. 'It's ridiculous, Liz! Do you know that? Bloody ridiculous!' He moved away to stare distractedly out of the window at the city stretching away into the distance, and Liz knew that she had caused him a great deal of pain. He had often appeared to be a frivolous, happy-go-lucky person, but it was clear that she had underestimated him, which made her rejection of his love even harder.

'Look, Liz,' he said, turning from the window with the air of a man who had made an important decision, 'I accept that you think you don't want me now, but that bastard doesn't care for you, you know, and I intend to be around when you realise that fact. I'll wait as long as I need to, Liz. You're not getting away from me so easily!'

'Oh, Andrew, it's no use!' Liz whispered tearfully. 'I wish I did love you instead of Francisco. Maybe it would have been different if I'd met you first, but it's too late now! Even though I know that Francisco won't come back,' she added sadly. 'I shall never love anyone but Francisco, and I shan't marry again.'

'Hell! You say that now, Liz, but give it six months and you'll wonder what you ever saw in the guy.'

'I wonder that you can love me if you have such a poor opinion of my fidelity,' Liz said sadly. 'Aren't you afraid that I would also tire of you in six months if we were married?'

'Don't be an idiot, love! There's no comparison between the two situations. Just say you'll let me hang around,' he added urgently, going down on his haunches beside her and taking her hands between his own. 'I love you and I'll do anything for you. Let me help you now, Liz.'

'I don't know what to say!' Liz shook her head distractedly, as though the action might help to straighten the confused jumble of her thoughts. 'I can't decide anything now. I would really like to be on my own, Andrew,' she added with sudden determination. 'I'll ring you if I need you—I promise.'

It was plain to see that Andrew was not satisfied with her decision, but he shrugged his shoulders with as good a grace as he could muster. 'O.K.! O.K., love, but if I don't hear from you soon I'll be back again—you can be sure of that,' he added steadily.

Liz rose to accompany him into the hall and finally closed the door behind him with a combination of relief and sadness.

CHAPTER TWO

FRANCISCO did not return to the flat after his abrupt departure. The only contact that she had with him was through the agency of the solicitors. They informed her that she could stay in the flat and that a very generous allowance would continue to be paid into her account each month. There was no mention of divorce, but Liz guessed that it would only be a matter of time before it occurred.

The solicitor's letter helped to make her accept the finality of her break with Francisco, and with acceptance came a glimmer of her old pride and determination to stand on her own two feet. She rang Andrew as soon as her decision was made, to tell him that there was no possibility of a future together for them. If he did not accept her decision as a final one, at least he made no immediate attempt to visit her again.

A decision about the flat and the allowance had been harder to reach, but Liz was determined not to take anything from Francisco if she could help it. His opinion of her as an opportunist who had married him for his money hardened her resolve. She would leave university and get a job—move away from London with its unhappy memories. She had managed successfully so far to avoid thinking about the effect on her parents of the break-up of her marriage. Her decision to leave university would be an added blow, but there seemed to be no practical alternative.

It was a few days after Francisco's departure before she finally plucked up courage to write to her parents and tell them the truth, and it was a rather blotched and tearful missive which she finally folded and put into the envelope

Hastily she donned her hooded raincoat and rushed out into the wet and blustery afternoon, only to see the G.P.O. van disappearing around the corner. She slipped the letter into the post box anyway and walked back to the flat, making no attempt to hurry out of the vicious wind which blew the rain in stinging slaps across her face, whipping her coat in angry folds around her legs.

She was forced to concede that the weather suited her mood. Anyone who did not know her would be forced to assume that her calm appearance denoted a lack of feeling, an absence of despair. The truth was that even with her life in ruins around her she was unable to give in, forced to keep up appearances if only for the sake of her pride.

The core of her being felt as though it was turned to stone. She woke frequently in the night, her pillow drenched with tears, and yet some inner force still compelled her to fight. Her father had the same fighting spirit, and Liz found herself wishing that she had not inherited the trait. It would be a blessed relief to give way to her grief and allow someone else to take charge—but it was not to be.

When she finally reached Templeton Court it was to see the porter urgently beckoning her.

'Oh, Mrs Ramirez, there's a telegram come for you, about two minutes ago—I was hoping you wouldn't be long. I hope it's not bad news ma'am,' he added, as he passed the envelope to her.

Fumbling in her bag, she handed him a tip, then, rather than open the envelope under his interested eye, she thanked him rather tremulously and hurried away to the flat on unsteady legs, a number of wild and unreasonable fantasies rushing through her mind.

She was so sure that the telegram must concern Francisco that when she finally read the message it took a few moments for the contents to register in her confused brain:

REGRET PARENTS HAD ACCIDENT STOP
COME IMMEDIATELY
ST WILFRED'S HOSPITAL
UNCLE BEN

For a moment the shock completely immobilised her and she sank heavily into a chair, closing her eyes against the unwelcome visions conjured up by the news. Dazedly she forced herself to move towards the phone. She must arrange a flight to Yeadon straight away. This was no time to break down—Mum and Dad needed her.

Later, as she sat in the taxi that hurried her to the airport, she had reason to bless Francisco's generosity and feel thankful that she had not been so foolish as to return the money he had already put into her bank account. Although she knew that she must try not to think about his generosity—she must remember his cruelty to her in the last few weeks and cling to the bitter thought that he ought to be here now, helping her, when she and her parents needed him.

When she reached St Wilfred's Hospital it was to discover that she was too late to see her father; he had died within an hour of being admitted to hospital. Later, when she looked back on this time, Liz wondered why she had not collapsed immediately when told the news. It was almost as though another person was in her shoes, performing the needed actions, so that she was calm and composed when the nurse took her in to see her mother.

'I'm glad you've come, love . . . I thought you might be too late. . . .'

'Oh, Mum!' Liz whispered in a choked little voice, 'don't say that! Hurry up and get well. You have to, I need you, Mum . . . we all need you.'

She had been determined not to cry, but found the sight of her mother's broken body in the clinical hospital bed too much to bear after all the other troubles of the past week.

'You've no need to pretend with me, love,' Mrs Hanson said quietly. 'I shouldn't know what to do with myself, living on now your dad's gone. If you and Francisco are half as happy as your dad and I have been, you'll be very lucky, Liz. I'm tired now, I think I'll have a little sleep,' her mother added, stretching out a comforting hand to grasp Liz's cold fingers. 'Sit with me for a while, love, if you can.'

'Yes, yes, of course I will, Mum—don't worry, I'll be here when you want me. Go to sleep if you're tired,' she added gently, stroking her mother's workworn hand.

'Liz! Liz! . . .'

'Yes, I'm here, Mum. Don't try to talk now—just rest.'

'I just wanted to say that I'm glad you've got Francisco to look after you. He's a good man . . . glad we let you marry him. Dad was worried, but we were right to let you . . . I'm glad,' she sighed wearily, and closed her eyes, her hand relaxing in Liz's clasp.

Liz spent the next few hours sitting quietly by her mother's bed, but she never spoke sensibly again. It was just after midnight when she died, and even though Liz knew that her mother had spoken the truth when she said she did not want to live without her husband, it was impossible not to shed many bitter tears. The irony of her mother's last words struck Liz forcibly. As though the double loss of her parents was not enough to bear, she was deprived of the love and support of Francisco's presence, and now she had to face the future completely alone.

She returned to stay in her parents' house until after the funeral, and although it seemed drab and shabby in comparison with the London flat, the well loved rooms closed around her with womblike warmth and familiar objects became doubly valued because of their association with her parents. A constant stream of old friends and relatives came to express their sympathy and with the help of pills from the doctor to make her sleep at night, there was little time to think or give way to grief.

Mrs Helliwell, her parents' next-door neighbour, urged her to give way to her tears. 'Don't bottle it up, love, have a good cry. It'll only be worse later if you don't. We all know how much you thought about your mum and dad, lass—Eh well,' she sniffed as tears came into her own eyes, 'we all thought a lot about them, that we did—there was no kinder chap than Fred. . . .'

She gave Liz's shoulders a gentle shake and said: 'When our Jean lost her husband she was just like you—wouldn't cry at first, but when she finally did she couldn't stop. She still hasn't got over it—not two years afterwards. Where's this husband of yours, I'd like to know?' she added abruptly with a sniff. 'Even if he's gone to Spain as you say—surely he could come home now—write to him, lass, ask him to come,' she urged. 'You need him here now. Apart from the fact that it wasn't right, him not being at the funeral. . . .'

The grief which Liz had so successfully kept at bay over the last two weeks became too violent for her to control. Tears began to flow down her cheeks, slowly and silently at first, until eventually her body began to shake with violent, racking sobs. Mrs Helliwell stared in consternation for a moment and then her face collapsed in ready sympathy. She stepped forward and drew Liz into the circle of her comforting arms.

'Eh, love, never heed what I say . . . my tongue fair runs away with me,' she murmured, stroking Liz's hair with a work hardened hand. 'Never mind, lass . . . you cry if you want to, it'll do you good.'

When the paroxysm of sobbing finally ended, Liz sat up rather shakily and Mrs Helliwell thrust a very large, clean handkerchief towards her. 'Here, love, use this. I've got another here,' she added patting the ample pockets of her blue apron.

'I'm sorry, Mrs Helliwell,' Liz said shakily, wiping her

eyes and blowing her nose fiercely. 'I don't know what came over me, I'm afraid I've soaked your cardigan.'

'Not to worry, love, you've not spoiled anything. I tell you what, I'm going to put the kettle on, I could do with a cuppa myself.'

Mrs Helliwell bustled noisily into the kitchen and the sound of clattering cups and saucers came to Liz's ears as she closed her eyes wearily and leaned her head back against the old moquette settee. She sat up again with a guilty start as Mrs Helliwell entered the room, a loaded tray in her hands, aware that she had been very close to sleep.

'Eh, love, did I disturb you? I'm sorry—still you're awake now, so we might as well have this tea,' she added, setting the tray down on the small walnut coffee table. 'You don't take sugar, do you, Liz?' she asked, handing Liz her cup and putting two large spoonfuls in her own cup before settling back comfortably into the fireside chair. Momentarily she seemed at a loss for words, but then— 'You ... er ... you might not want to answer this question, love, tell me to mind my own business if you want, I shan't be offended—but is there something wrong between you and that husband of yours?'

The words sounded hard and intrusive even to Mrs Helliwell's own ears and Liz stared at her teacup steadily for a few moments, until she had regained her composure. Then she raised her eyes and smiled tremulously at her kindly neighbour, knowing that the question had not been asked in a prying spirit but purely out of a desire to help.

'If you'd asked me that question a couple of days ago I think I would have been unwilling to answer it,' Liz said. 'But now I think I need to talk. I must tell someone! I don't think I can keep it to myself any longer.'

'Tell me if it will help, Liz—it'll not go any farther, that I can swear,' she said.

Mrs Helliwell was not as surprised or shocked as Liz had expected; nor was she inclined to put the blame on anyone's shoulders.

'It would have surprised me if you *had* managed to make a success of the marriage, and that's a fact. Even without this business with the young lad, I can't see it would have lasted long,' she added, squeezing Liz's hand sympathetically, in mute apology for her uncompromising words. 'Love at first sight is all very well for romantic stories, but it's fair difficult to live with. You both expected too much from each other, Liz, it was obvious you would have problems. You both being from different backgrounds—him foreign and having all that money,' she added rather disparagingly. 'It didn't help, either, you being only seventeen, did it, love? I told your dad ... still, never mind that,' she added quickly. 'What's past is past.' After a moment she went on, 'It isn't as though that husband of yours was young and inexperienced, he was old enough to know he would have to tread carefully, I should have thought. Still, he was foreign!' she said with a sniff, as though that explained everything.

'It wasn't only Francisco's fault! I was thoughtless ... very thoughtless. . . .'

'I'm not saying it was, Liz! I can see you did some daft things, but don't we all? I should think that most of what went wrong was due to circumstances beyond your control, as they say, and all you can do now is put it behind you, try to build a new life,' Mrs Helliwell added. 'There'll be plenty of young men around when you're ready for them—you'll see! The thing to do first is to build up your strength—like a shadow you are,' she said, staring critically at Liz's over slim figure and gaunt face. 'You leave everything to me and don't worry,' she soothed, patting Liz's hands in a motherly fashion.

Mrs Helliwell was true to her word and took complete charge of Liz—arranging for her to have a break from university and giving her the moral support she needed as she tried to plan for the future. But within a month of her parents' deaths Liz realised that she would have to come to terms with additional complications in her life. She could no longer avoid the obvious conclusions—her body was not functioning normally and it could no longer be put down to shock or worry. She just had to accept the fact that she was pregnant—she was going to have Francisco's baby!

It was a bleak and cold Saturday morning when she finally faced the unpalatable facts, and the weather suited her mood of utter helplessness. She knew that subconsciously this was why she had not made any firm decisions about the future: there was no need to! Once Francisco knew that she was going to have his child he would take her back. . . . Oh, not because he loved her, Liz thought bitterly, but to satisfy his own family feeling and his wish for an heir.

He definitely wouldn't consider her fit to care for his child. Dear God!—she caught her breath in horror as a new thought struck her—perhaps he would even take the child away from her, let his mother care for it. In her agitation at this thought she began to pace around the kitchen, fantastic plans for hiding from Francisco running through her brain. It was no good—no good at all. If she disappeared from his life completely he was sure to become suspicious, sure to trace her, and then what? No, that wasn't the solution; but there must be some way for her to keep the child. She stopped her agitated pacing and held her hands over her stomach with fiercely possessive pride—there must be some way. . . .

'Liz! Liz, are you up yet? Shall I make you some tea, love?'

'Oh, Mrs Helliwell. . . .' Liz broke off distractedly, rubbing her forehead with agitated fingers.

'Whatever's the matter now, lass? You look fair hot and bothered!'

Mrs Helliwell's prosaic manner served to steady Liz's jangling nerves. She must confide in someone and Mrs

Helliwell had been such a good friend already that she could have no doubts about trusting her.

'Well, love, I just don't know what to suggest, that I don't,' Mrs Helliwell sighed, when Liz had spilled out her new problems. Her motherly face was marred by a worried frown and she shook her head in dismay, overcome by this new addition to Liz's many burdens. 'As if you didn't have enough on your plate as it is. . . . Well, it never rains but it pours,' she added philosophically. 'I think here's where we need an extra set of brains—our Sam will mebbe know what to suggest. Don't you worry, Liz, we'll think of something. A baby, eh—it'll be fair grand having another little 'un around,' she murmured to herself as she hurried towards the door.

Sam was a small man, inevitably dressed in immaculate grey flannels and a spotless white shirt and as slim as Mrs Helliwell was plump. Liz always felt that Mrs Helliwell was about to pick him up and tuck him under her arm as she would a recalcitrant grandchild, or pop him into her capacious apron pocket. He had suffered a stroke two years before and walked with a slight limp, but his mind was as sharp and active as when he had worked at the betting office in the town centre, and he soon had a possible solution to Liz's problem.

'Well, Mrs Ramirez, the way I see it. . . .'

'Give over, Sam!' Mrs Helliwell interrupted impatiently. 'What's all this Mrs Ramirez business? You'll be calling me Mrs Helliwell next, I shouldn't wonder,' she added indignantly.

'Yes, please call me Liz. . . .'

'All right then, lass, Liz it is—but you'd better call me Sam, none of this Mr Helliwell lark, or I'll be getting to feel like a pensioner,' he added with a sly grin at his wife.

'Oh, you . . . get on with you! Never mind the blarney, Sam Helliwell! Tell us what you've decided. You wouldn't think it, Liz,' said Mrs Helliwell, trying to hide her obvious pride in her husband behind her raillery, 'but our

Sam has a decent set of brains when he can stop his tongue rattling on and get down to using them.'

'Yes, well, Liz, as I was saying before I was so rudely interrupted . . . the way I see it, you must let your husband know you're expecting a child. You think he'd find out anyway, even if you tried to hide the fact—right?'

'Yes, I think he would.'

'Yes . . . well! This Francisco thinks you've been carrying on with a lad from university,' he hurried on without waiting for Liz's acquiescence. 'It seems to me if you're sure you don't want Francisco to take you and the baby back, that if Francisco believed the baby was this Andrew's, you wouldn't have any problems—right?'

'But the baby isn't Andrew's,' Liz explained wearily. 'And I could never say it was—not to Francisco, not even now. I wouldn't give him that satisfaction!'

'Nay, but you wouldn't have to—say it, I mean,' Sam added as he caught her puzzled look. 'If your husband's as jealous and pigheaded as you say, it will be enough to write and tell him you're having a baby, without saying whose. I should think he'll jump to the obvious conclusion.'

'The obvious conclusion to anyone but Francisco would be that the baby was his,' said Liz with a flash of spirit. 'It will just add fuel to the flames of his suspicions.'

'Aye, that's right, it will,' Sam agreed. 'But you can't have it both ways.' He took her hands in his own thin grasp and squeezed them reassuringly. 'He already seems certain that you've been unfaithful, and you say you don't want the risk of him taking the baby away—this is the only solution as far as I can see.'

'You're right, Sam, I know that! It's just that it will seem like admitting that his suspicions were justified from the beginning.'

'Well now, that's settled!' interrupted Mrs Helliwell before Liz had time to dwell on the possible repercussions of her decision. 'Now I think you need to decide straight away what you're going to do about university, where you'll live. . . .'

'Yes, I suppose so.' Liz ran her fingers distractedly through her already tumbled hair. 'I don't need to work, of course. Francisco has arranged for me to have an allowance, and I don't think he'll stop that, even when he knows about the baby. It would go against his family pride to know that his wife was in need,' she explained bitterly. 'It's not that he really cares what happens to me!'

She rose hastily and began to walk around the room as though the movement would help her to think and plan for the future, looking totally unlike a mother-to-be, in jeans which hung loosely around her slender hips, never hinting at the new life already burgeoning in her slim body.

'The fact is that I don't want to accept Francisco's money. Do you know, he thinks I married him for his money?' she added, turning to look at Mrs Helliwell.

'Nay lass, then he's a fool!' Mrs Helliwell said vigorously.

'Excuse me asking,' Sam interrupted a little hesitantly. 'I know it's none of my business, but didn't your dad leave you any brass, Liz? I'm sure he had a nest egg put by,' he added, before either of his bewildered audience could interrupt him. 'He told me, not more than a year ago—just before you met that Francisco—that if your mum was left a widow she'd be all right. I don't know how much, like—but I reckon he had a few thousand; and the house was his own. . . .' His voice trailed away as he saw the blank incomprehension on Liz's face. 'Has the solicitor said nowt to you, lass?'

'No . . . no . . . he asked me to go and see him, I just haven't got around to it.' She shook her head expressively. 'I didn't know Dad owned the house. I thought it was rented. I wondered why no one had come to ask me for the money, I thought he must have paid a month at a

time. I was going to ask you about it, Mrs Helliwell,' she
added in a bewildered voice.

'Well, love, that settles it,' said Mrs Helliwell. 'You go
on to the phone box at the end of the road, ring the
solicitor and make an appointment for this afternoon if
you can, and see what he has to say. You can settle your
other problems when you know how you stand about
money.'

A few hours later Liz was standing, looking totally bewildered, in the kitchen of the Helliwell house. She had
changed into the only decent item of clothing that she
had brought with her for her visit to the solicitor, and the
dark chocolate brown of the trouser suit enhanced her
pallor and hung on her slender frame with inches to
spare.

'It's unbelievable . . . it really is,' she told them. 'I told
the solicitor that I thought there'd been a mistake, but he
assures me there isn't. Dad did own the house and he also
left a substantial sum of money. The solicitor thinks he
had a win on the pools in the last few years and that he
saved the rest out of his pension from work, though how
he could afford to I just don't know.' She sank heavily
into a chair as Mrs Helliwell urged her towards it and
leaned her head wearily on her hands.

'You don't think...,' Mrs Helliwell said hesitantly. 'No,
never mind, lass, it was nothing, just a thought....'

'Please, Mrs Helliwell, tell me!'

'Do you think that your husband could have given Fred
money? I know your dad was a proud man, but still, he
had responsibilities.'

'No, no, Mrs Helliwell—I thought of that at first; but I
made Francisco promise not to offer Dad money. I knew
it would make him angry. Dad told me when Francisco
and I were married that he was pleased Francisco hadn't
offered him money—he said he liked him better for not
doing so. I told Dad that if ever he or Mum needed any-

thing they only had to ask—I told Mum too, I knew she wouldn't let pride stand in her way if they were really stuck. So you see, it couldn't be that,' Liz said quietly. 'The solicitor seemed sure about the pools win, and it is quite likely, I suppose. It's just odd that they never mentioned it.'

She turned troubled eyes towards Mrs Helliwell's homely countenance. 'Well, love, I don't know why you're looking so worried,' Mrs Helliwell said reassuringly. 'As far as I can see your money troubles are over and you can tell that husband of yours to stick his allowance up his jumper,' she added inelegantly.

Liz was surprised into a quiet laugh and Mrs Helliwell commented: 'That's the first time I've heard you laugh since the accident! You mark my words, love, things can only get better. Now stir your bones and help to set the table for tea, it's stew and dumplings, and I know you like that. Of course you're staying,' she added as Liz would have interrupted her. 'It's my job to put some meat on your bones—you've got to eat for two now, m'dear, and don't you forget. Aye, and you'd better go to the doctor's in the morning, just to make sure. Then you can write to that husband of yours and tell him the news.'

Sam had been correct in his reading of Francisco's character. When Liz informed him, through the medium of his solicitor, that she was expecting a child, he automatically assumed that Andrew Mellor was the father: and any guilt that Liz had felt about the phrasing of her letter to Francisco was banished when she received his damning reply. He was not willing to give her the benefit of the doubt, it seemed, and although her allowance would continue he made it very clear that he never wished to see either her or the child in the future.

It gave Liz a great deal of bitter satisfaction to write and assure the solicitor that she did not intend to accept Francisco's allowance and also ask them to re-let the flat as she would no longer be using it.

The next months were a strange time for Liz. Although her circumstances seemed so hopeless she never gave way to despair and continued to present a reasonably cheerful face to the world. The sharp angles of her body filled out as her pregnancy advanced and her hair had never been so glossy, nor her skin so petal-soft.

To a casual observer she appeared the model of contented womanhood. Yet when she visited the doctor there was no loving husband waiting to collect her, and she had begun to dread the inevitable stay in hospital after the birth, when she would undoubtedly be the subject of much interested gossip.

In the event she need not have worried. Edward arrived with so little fuss and Liz felt so well that the doctor accepted Mrs Helliwell's assurance that she would look after Liz and the baby and had allowed her home after forty-eight hours.

As Liz lay in bed holding the small sleeping form of Edward, she knew that she could never allow him to be taken from her; and all traces of guilt at having deceived Francisco finally disappeared. Looking down at the downy black head and the little face relaxed in sleep, she was surprised at the flood of maternal feeling which surged through her. Snuggling close to the sweet-smelling bundle, she vowed she would fight tooth and nail to keep the child and bring him up herself. Whatever the future might bring she and Edward were going to be together, on that she was determined.

CHAPTER THREE

Liz peered out of the train window, trying to recognise any familiar landmarks. They weren't too far from London now, another twenty minutes and she would be there. John had not wanted her to come, of course, but the solicitor had advised her to make the journey and he had finally agreed.

Liz smiled warmly to herself as she thought of John Spencer. He was everything that Francisco had never been—kind and gentle, with laughing eyes and a wonderful sense of humour. She had met him as soon as she had gone as secretary to Parkheaton Comprehensive School where he was head of the languages department. He had been a great help to her in her work during that first term, and at the same time had plainly shown that he was interested in her as a woman. She had discouraged him at first, not wishing to become involved again after her disastrous marriage, but the warmth of his personality had won her over, and now here she was asking Francisco for a divorce so that she could marry John.

It should be an ideal marriage, she thought happily. They had known each other for almost four years and they were both mature enough to know what they wanted. Their interests were very similar and, most important of all, John was very fond of Edward, a feeling that Edward reciprocated, Liz thought thankfully. If there was not the same magic when she was in his arms—well, perhaps that was a good thing, it was that special magic that had caused many of the problems in her first marriage. They would probably have more chance of success without it, Liz thought ruefully.

The train jerked to a stop with a squeal of brakes and

Liz glanced quickly at her watch. They were early into King's Cross, so she should have plenty of time to get to the solicitors' office. Perhaps she could even have a quick look at some of the dress shops in Oxford Street. She looked down ruefully at her cream linen trouser suit. It had most certainly seen better days, but there was little money to spare for her own wardrobe. Edward was growing at such a rate that she had difficulty making sure that he was adequately clothed.

She was quite unaware that today she was looking particularly beautiful, her thick blonde hair drawn into a knot on top of her head, a few long tendrils inadvertently escaping around her ears, and although the suit she was wearing was in its fourth season, it emphasised her light golden tan and well shaped figure beautifully.

She left the train and after walking through the barrier went into the temporarily deserted ladies' room. She grimaced critically at her reflection in the cloakroom mirror. She would have to do, but she didn't exactly look the part—estranged or otherwise—of the wife of a member of Spain's wealthy aristocracy. Well, she wouldn't be for long, and there was absolutely no need to feel nervous about her coming interview with Messrs Launceston, Launceston and Sellerman. With that thought she stiffened her shoulders mentally and left the cloakroom, heading towards the fashion shops and an hour's window-shopping.

At two-thirty precisely she arrived outside the solicitors' office, wondering for at least the twentieth time why they had so specifically asked to see her, why everything could not have been sorted out by them and her own solicitor. Oh well, she was going to find out now, wasn't she?

Taking a deep breath to steady her nerves, she pushed open the plate glass doors and walked, with more confidence than she was feeling, over the lush pile of the carpet towards the very elegant receptionist. She had barely time to sit in the seat to which she was shown, before she was being ushered into a large and luxuriously appointed office.

'Good afternoon, Señora Ramirez! May I introduce myself? I am Mr Launceston Senior.' The tall grey-haired man smiled coolly at her, and after shaking hands said: 'Please let me introduce my colleagues for the occasion.'

Liz looked around at the other occupants of the room. 'Oh! For a moment I thought. . . .' She paled visibly under her tan as Mr Launceston interrupted her smoothly.

'I don't believe you've met your husband's younger brother, Señor Carlos Ramirez.' Liz shook hands rather shakily with this younger version of Francisco, and as she did so Mr Sellerman, Mr Launceston's partner, moved forward to be introduced.

'Please, come and sit down, *señora*, then we can get down to the business of why we asked you to come here.'

As Liz took a seat she was conscious of Carlos Ramirez' intent regard and she turned to look at him with a questioning lift of her brows. He immediately turned away and she saw a slight flush rising beneath the dark tan of his face. Well, he certainly didn't have Francisco's overweening self-assurance, however like him he was in appearance. She could not remember Francisco ever losing his composure, except in moments of anger, of course.

Mr Launceston looked hesitantly towards Carlos Ramirez and said: 'Would you like to tell Señora Ramirez why we have asked her to come here, or shall I?'

'You, please, Mr Launceston!' he said quickly.

'Very well! Señora Ramirez. . . .' he hesitated a moment as though uncertain of how best to phrase his next words. 'Your husband wishes to put a proposition to you. There are certain matters that he would like to discuss with you before you take further steps towards divorce. He is willing to settle a substantial sum of money upon you, if you concede to those wishes.'

Liz stared rather blankly at the three men. 'I'm afraid

I don't quite understand,' she said finally. 'Why should Francisco want to see me now? After deserting me and then presumably putting me completely out of his mind for—what?' she hesitated, 'almost nine years.'

Mr Launceston cleared his throat apologetically. 'As to that, Señora Ramirez, there is a certain amount of doubt as to which partner committed the desertion. . . .'

Liz interrupted him angrily: 'I beg your pardon, Mr Launceston, but there is absolutely no doubt at all about the matter! Francisco told me that he intended to leave me—he left the flat and I've never seen him since. If that doesn't constitute desertion then I'm damned if I know what does!'

There was a momentary silence and then Mr Sellerman said: 'There was a child, I understand—not a product of your marriage to Señor Ramirez?'

'As to that, Francisco chooses to think that Edward is not his son. . . .'

'This is surely not the question at issue at the moment!' put in Carlos Ramirez, casting a sharp glance at Mr Sellerman. 'The question is whether or not you would be willing to see Francisco again, before taking further action towards divorce?'

'Of course!' said Liz. 'I'll see him if he wishes it, although what he hopes to gain I really don't know. Is he in London at the moment?' she asked, turning to look at Francisco's younger brother. 'Does he want to see me today?'

'Er—no, *señora*, my brother is not in England at the moment. This is the main problem! Pressure of business is such just now that he is unable to leave Spain. This question of divorce has come at the most awkward possible moment, as Francisco is planning to widen the American markets for our wines.'

'I'm so sorry I didn't choose a more convenient time for Francisco!' Liz said acidly.

Carlos began to look a little embarrassed and moved

uncomfortably in his seat.

'I did not mean to imply a criticism; I was merely stating the facts—explaining why Francisco wishes you to go to Spain to see him. He will pay all your expenses, of course!' he added hastily, as he saw the look of refusal written plainly on her face.

'I'm very grateful to Francisco for the long-delayed invitation to visit him in Spain; but I haven't the slightest intention of doing so. If this was your only reason for asking me here then I'm afraid you've wasted both my time and yours.' Liz began to gather her bag and gloves together, intending to leave the office as quickly as possible. The meeting had disturbed her more than she cared to admit, and the shock of seeing Carlos Ramirez, in particular, had further upset her already jangled nerves.

'If you remember, *señora*, I said there were two propositions to consider,' Mr Launceston put in smoothly.

'Yes, I do remember. You said Francisco was willing to settle a generous sum of money on me, if I conceded to his demands,' Liz answered, turning to look at Mr Launceston. They were the typical solicitors for Francisco to choose, she thought ruefully. Almost as self-assured and arrogant as he was himself, and just as convinced that money was all powerful.

'His wishes, *señora* . . . if you accede to his wishes!' Carlos Ramirez said quickly.

Liz shot him a look. 'Very well—wishes, if you prefer that word. But as I have no intention of agreeing with either his wishes or his demands I can't see how this proposition could be of any interest to me! Also,' she added, beginning to warm to her theme, 'I do feel it's a little late for Francisco to concern himself with my welfare, financial or otherwise. I assure you that I've managed perfectly well without his assistance over the last nine years; and I have every intention of continuing to do so. Good afternoon, gentlemen!' She inclined her head briefly, walked quickly to the door and down the steps before the three men had time to gather their scattered wits.

However, as she walked along the busy street, gazing unseeingly into shop windows and trying to steady her disordered nerves, she heard hurried footsteps behind her and her arm was grasped insistently. She was forced to turn and look into the flustered face of Carlos Ramirez.

'I hoped I would find you!' he gasped, slightly breathless after his exertions. 'I would like to have further conversation with you, if you will permit me?'

Liz moved impatiently out of his grasp. 'I have no intention of returning to the solicitor's office, Señor Ramirez, so I'm afraid this has been a wasted exercise!'

'Please! Will you come with me somewhere for a coffee? Somewhere quiet where we can talk without being disturbed!'

Liz felt herself weakening rapidly. He seemed very young and vulnerable in this mood and something about him caught at her heartstrings in a most disturbing way. It must be his likeness to Edward, she decided; he did look very much like a small boy with his hair tousled from running. Involuntarily she gave him a smile.

'Why, you are perfectly beautiful,' Carlos said quickly.

Liz found herself laughing and shaking her head in amusement she said: 'Well, I certainly can't refuse to have coffee with you after that lovely compliment! I'd forgotten how flattering Spanish men could be!'

'It was perfectly sincere,' he assured her earnestly. 'I did not say it to make you come with me—although I do wish to speak to you very much.'

The coffee house they eventually found was not very quiet, but their table was in a small alcove shielded by tall-backed seats, so that it was possible to have a reasonably private conversation.

After the waitress had walked away, Carlos said: 'I am sorry I made such a personal remark to you just now. I hope you are not offended with me?'

'How could I be when the remark was such a flattering

one?' Liz smiled again, feeling her liking for him deepening.

'I did not mean it to be flattering! You are beautiful—very beautiful! I had not realised just how much until you smiled at me. How Francisco could bear ... however, that is not my business,' he said, after a moment's hesitation. 'I wanted to ask you to reconsider your decision not to go to Spain. Francisco is most anxious to speak to you, and I assure you that the settlement would make it well worth your while—it would be very generous, you understand!'

'Yes, yes, I understand very well!' Liz shrugged her shoulders wearily. 'I understand that Francisco is, as usual, determined to get his own way whatever the cost. However, I'm now in the fortunate position of not having to listen to his demands at close quarters, so the answer must be no. Very definitely no!'

Carlos stared at her in amazement. 'Are you not just a little bit afraid of defying him? I must confess that when he is angry with me, he makes me—how do you say—shiver in my shoes—*si*?'

'Well, you know, Carlos ... er ... may I call you Carlos?' As he assented with a smile she continued: 'He can't really do anything to me now, can he? And I don't really think he will bother to make the effort. Besides,' she added a little ruefully, 'I expect he got quite used to my defying him when we were living together. I seemed to do little else towards the end of the marriage.'

'Do you hate him very much? Is that why you won't go to Spain?'

'No, I don't hate him—not now, anyway; and I would be willing to meet him if he came to England. But I don't see why I should put myself out, going all the way to Spain, when it's he who wants to see me. Apart from anything else the memories that I have of my only visit to Spain in Francisco's company are not particularly pleasant ones.'

'I expect my parents were a little cool with you? *Si!* It was nothing personal, you understand, just that they had hoped Francisco would marry the daughter of one of our neighbours. They were naturally disappointed,' Carlos added apologetically. 'There are only the children living on the estate at the moment. Padre died some time ago, and Madre is living with her sister near Madrid—for the company, you understand. My youngest sister is away at school much of the time and my other sisters are married and widely scattered. Francisco and I are the only members of the family living permanently on the estate.'

There was a moment's silence as Liz looked curiously at Carlos. 'Just how far is Francisco willing to go to get his own way? Just how large a sum of money is he prepared to bribe me with?'

'I was told to offer you in the region of ten thousand pounds.'

Liz gave a loud gasp. 'He must be mad! You mean I was to have that sum just for visiting Spain? I should think it would have been much cheaper to allow his American business to drift for the moment and come to England himself for a couple of days!'

'He must not think so,' Carlos said quietly. 'You are then still determined to turn down the offer? You will not come to Spain?'

'No, I won't come. I'm sorry if it makes things difficult for you.'

'I will of course have to explain the matter to Francisco.' Carlos shrugged his shoulders expressively. 'However, I am used to facing his displeasure. I am his partner in the business, you understand, and he is sometimes . . . difficult to please.'

'I just bet he is!' Liz said with feeling. 'Poor Carlos! I do feel a brute. But I really have no wish to go to Spain to see Francisco, either now or in the future.' She glanced quickly at her watch, and added, 'Look, I must go, I'm afraid. I intended to catch the train at four-thirty, and I mustn't be late. I have to collect Edward from a friend's house.'

'Edward?' Carlos looked questioningly at her and Liz felt the telltale colour flooding into her cheeks.

'Edward is my son. Francisco told you that I had a son, didn't he?' she asked.

'Yes, yes. I knew of your son, but I had forgotten for the moment,' he added apologetically.

'As a matter of interest, just what is Edward supposed to do while I'm in Spain?' asked Liz. 'I presume that even though he bears the proud name of Ramirez he will not be allowed into the family home ... hm?' Before Carlos could answer she continued: 'How Francisco can bear to invite a ... a ... fallen woman such as myself into his home, I really don't know. Isn't he afraid that I might pollute the place?'

Carlos cleared his throat nervously. 'Er ... Francisco has arranged to make money available to pay someone to care for the boy during your visit—don't worry, everything would be taken care of, Liz,' he added placatingly, shooting a glance at the neighbouring tables to see whether Liz's angry words had been overheard.

'Money again! I might have known,' Liz sighed. 'Oh, don't worry, Carlos,' she added as she saw the direction of his gaze. 'No one is in the least interested in us—that's one of the attractions of London, one can be anonymous at times. Look, I must go now. I hope Francisco won't be too angry with you. ...'

He shrugged philosophically. 'Don't worry, I will be fine. If you should change your mind about the visit, you have only to contact the solicitor and all the necessary arrangements will be made.'

They walked out of the coffee house together and Liz held out her hand. 'It hasn't been a wasted journey after all, Carlos. I'm so very glad to have met you.'

He drew her hand to his lips and placed a warm kiss on her fingers. 'The pleasure has been all mine! I confess that I hoped you would come to Spain for purely selfish reasons. I would like to see you again . . . perhaps I could visit you when I am in this country again on business?' he asked a little hesitantly.

'Better not, I think,' Liz said quietly. '*Adios*, Carlos.'

'*Buena suerte*, Liz. I hope everything goes well for you. Go now—you must not miss your train.'

When Liz woke the next morning she was beset by doubts as to whether she had been sensible to refuse Francisco's offer. If, as she had told Carlos, she did not mind meeting Francisco again, surely it was foolish of her to turn down the visit to Spain and the subsequent money settlement. It was true that she did not want the money for herself, but had she the right to refuse it when she had Edward to consider?

She sighed and turned restlessly on to her stomach among the rumpled bedcovers. John would support them both happily, of course, but she knew that he did not want her to go on working after they were married, and as they both wanted more children, money would be fairly tight. Liz lay wrestling with a disturbingly guilty conscience. Edward had had plenty of love and understanding in his short life, but very little in the way of material benefits. If she accepted the money from Francisco she would also have the satisfaction of knowing that her son would not be a drain on John's slender resources.

Insidiously, grave doubts began to creep into her mind. Had she made the correct decision at Edward's birth? Should she have made a determined effort to force Francisco to accept that he was the father of her son? She had to admit that the life she and Francisco had led together would not have been good for her son. It would have been difficult for him, living with parents who quarrelled constantly.

She was forced to put her worries to one side for the moment, as the subject of her thoughts poked a bright face around the bedroom door.

'Come on, Mum, hurry up and get breakfast! I promised to meet Chris and David for a game of football at half past nine.'

'Oh no, Edward!' Liz groaned loudly. 'Not more muddy shorts and socks! I must have washed at least five lots last week.'

Edward grinned at her, and Liz was struck anew with his likeness to his father, with his thick dark hair and long eyelashes, and the deep tan which he seemed to acquire without any effort. No one who saw them together would be able to doubt their relationship.

'It hasn't rained for a few days, so perhaps we won't get too dirty,' Edward said in a conciliating tone.

'That will definitely be too much to expect! Why can't you have a nice clean hobby like swimming?' Liz sighed as she moved reluctantly out of bed. 'Go out now, darling, and you can start setting the table. I'll have a quick wash and come down straight away. I can have my bath later in peace and quiet,' she added with a smile.

Over breakfast Edward seemed a little preoccupied. 'Are you feeling quite well, Edward?' Liz asked, looking anxiously at him.

'What?—Oh! Yes, of course, Mum. I was just thinking. . . .'

'I see, that sounds ominous,' commented Liz, pushing her plate to one side and leaning her elbows on the table rather inelegantly. 'Well, aren't you going to tell me?'

'Mmm,' said Edward uncertainly. 'I quite see that it won't be possible for this to happen, so perhaps I shouldn't mention it . . . Only it was with you saying couldn't I have a clean hobby, you see.'

Liz shot him a quizzical glance. 'I presume there's something you'd like to do, only it will cost money, is that it?'

'Yes—well, I've always wanted to learn to ride—I was looking at a book about Andalucia the other day. They have some marvellous horses there,' he said enthusiastically.

Liz stiffened slightly. 'Why were you looking at a book about Spain, love?'

Edward shifted a little uncomfortably in his seat, but continued bravely, 'Well, you told me that Father was born there, so I just thought I'd see what it was like. I wanted to show Chris too,' he added hesitantly. 'He was asking about my father, where he came from and everything.'

'Edward, your father is dead. I don't really think it's a good idea to start delving into the past!' Liz softened slightly as she saw the downcast look on his face. 'Look, if it makes you happy, I promise that as soon as there's any money to spare we'll find a riding school for you—although it won't be next week—or next month,' she added as she saw the look of excitement on his face.

'It doesn't matter, Mum, it will be something to look forward to!' He finished his breakfast hastily, still managing to devour three large slices of toast dripping with honey. 'I must dash now—I'm going to be late!' he said, bundling his football kit into an untidy parcel on his way through the door. 'See you at lunch, Mum!'

' 'Bye, Edward,' she called to his departing back. 'If I'm not at home when you get back I shall be at John's! Boys!' she muttered with feeling. Had he heard what she said or not? She smiled quietly to herself as she stacked the dishes. She had no need to worry about Edward, he was a very sensible boy, but also reassuringly normal; and his conversation at breakfast had solved one of her problems. She would have to accept Francisco's offer, if only for the sake of her son.

Carlos had said that she must ring the solicitor if she changed her mind, and that was a task that she did not look forward to. John would also have to know her decision and she had an awful feeling that he would not be very pleased.

What a morning! She sighed audibly as she washed the last of the dishes and left them to drain. She would go and see John as soon as she had bathed and she could ring the solicitor from his flat.

John, as she had expected, was not pleased about her decision to go to Spain. 'Are you sure you haven't the smallest subconscious hope that you and Francisco will get together again?' He gripped her shoulders gently, his eyes searching her face for some hint of her thoughts.

'Oh, don't be an idiot, love! I hate the man! Can you honestly think I have any reason to want him back again? He deserted me six months after our marriage and left me to bring up our son entirely on my own.'

'Aren't you forgetting something?' John said gently. 'Your husband doesn't realise that Edward is his son, and I feel quite sure, from what you've told me about him, that he would never have left you had he realised the true situation.'

'No, you're right there,' Liz agreed with un-characteristic bitterness. 'At least he wouldn't have left me until after the birth, and then he would no doubt have taken the baby too!'

'Don't go, Liz!' John said quietly, moving away from her to stare broodingly out of the window.

'But the money, John ... it's just too much to turn down in the circumstances. He can't eat me, after all,' she said with an uncertain laugh.

'I don't suppose he'll succeed in bullying you to do something you don't really want to do; but might not this visit make a divorce more difficult to obtain? You've been separated for nine years now, surely you want to be free as quickly as possible now that we've decided to marry? I want us to be able to marry soon,' he said in husky tones, leaving his place by the window and crossing the room to her side. He drew Liz into his arms and kissed her tenderly, and it was with a real sense of regret that Liz said:

'If I only had myself to consider I wouldn't even think about the offer—you know that, darling. I feel guilty about Edward, sorry that he's missed so much that should have been his by right. I never accepted money from Francisco when we separated, and this money will mean that Edward will never be a drain on your resources. . . .'

'My God, Liz,' John interrupted angrily, 'do you think I'd find him an unnecessary expense? I love the boy—just as I love you. Damn it, I want to provide for him!'

'I know, love, don't be angry.' Liz moved closer to him and smiled pleadingly into his eyes. 'It's just that I want Edward to have some of the material benefits that he would have had if we'd lived with Francisco.'

'As to that, I've maintained all along that you should have told your husband that Edward is his son, without trying to dissemble in any way. From what you tell me he would only have to look at the boy to see the truth.' John shrugged expressively. 'As you haven't done so I think you should be prepared to go it alone—put the man completely out of your life.'

'But that's exactly what I intend to do—after this visit there won't ever be any reason to contact him again, and we can forget him completely.'

'What? With his ten thousand pounds in the bank account?' John's tone was dry as he added, 'I should think he'll come very strongly to mind every time you spend some of the money.' He shrugged his shoulders philosophically. 'If you're so anxious to accept Francisco's offer I shan't try to stop you. I only hope we don't all live to regret your decision!'

CHAPTER FOUR

Liz felt very weary. She had left home at six this morning and worry about the coming meeting, combined with a restless night, was beginning to take its toll. They had reached the environs of Madrid and the stewardess had instructed them to fasten their seat-belts as a prelude to landing. Liz shivered inwardly. She had only flown a few times, but this was always the moment she feared. She gripped her hands together tightly and closed her eyes as the plane circled the airfield and came in towards the landing strip.

She tried to still the feeling of rising panic. She still had another flight to face today, and if she did not pull herself together soon, she would be a nervous wreck before she reached Seville. Her mind slipped back to that other journey to Spain ten years ago, when she had travelled with Francisco. It was the only time she had really enjoyed a flight. He made her fears seem quite ridiculous. . . .

She was suddenly aware of concentrated movements around her, and realised that the plane had landed without incident. She breathed a sigh of relief and rose, hesitantly, to join the other passengers as they moved towards the door.

She felt that now they had landed it would have been pleasant to spend a few hours in Madrid sightseeing, but the internal Iberia plane to Seville left within the hour, and there would be barely enough time to tidy herself before she had to catch it.

As she stepped out of the plane the heat from the tarmac hit her like a physical blow. She was forced to concede that the idea of sightseeing had not been such a good one.

Madrid at the beginning of August was not the most comfortable place to be. She realised that Seville would be equally hot, but as this was not a sightseeing trip it probably wouldn't matter very much.

Liz gave a mental shrug. She could not imagine Francisco taking time away from his American business concerns in order to show her the sights.

The line of passengers waiting to pass the barriers moved slowly, and she had only enough time to tidy her hair and freshen her face before boarding the plane to Seville. She knew that it took around two hours, so she should be in Seville by the middle of the afternoon.

The solicitor had told her that someone would be waiting at the airport to meet her. It would be pleasant if it was Carlos, but she could not prevent a feeling of dread that Francisco would be her welcoming committee. She could not imagine enjoying the drive to the estate in his sole company: although as the purpose of the visit was to talk to Francisco, the sooner the first steps were taken the easier the rest of the stay would be.

In spite of these bracing thoughts she found herself gazing with trepidation at the group of people waiting to meet the plane. She quickly scanned the faces and breathed a sigh of relief, Francisco definitely was not there, but her relief was abruptly dissipated as she saw the tall, dark figure walking towards the barrier. No, no— it was Carlos! She gave her husband's brother a dazzling smile, causing at least three of the men waiting at the barrier to cast Carlos looks of undisguised envy.

Carlos gazed with pleasure at Liz's slim figure as she waved to him. She was even more beautiful than he remembered; in her simple denim skirt and short-sleeved blouse, with her hair bound into a knot at the nape of her neck, she looked cool and elegant and altogether desirable. Francisco was a fool! What an idiot to marry a gorgeous creature like Liz and then to let her get away from him so easily.

'Liz! It's wonderful to see you!' Carlos smiled into her warm blue eyes.

'I was hoping it would be you who came to meet me, Carlos. I'm very glad to see you again too.' Carlos lifted her hand to his lips and kissed it warmly, drawing it companionably through his arm as he escorted her through the departure lounge and towards the waiting car. He opened the door of the gleaming, silver monster that awaited them, settled Liz into the front passenger seat and stowed her case in the capacious trunk, climbing in beside her and slamming the door firmly behind him.

'Lovely!' Liz stretched luxuriously on the comfortable seat. 'This is a Rolls-Royce, isn't it?'

'Yes,' Carlos laughed. 'Oh, it's not mine. Francisco was intending to meet you, but he was called away on business at the last moment. He insisted that I should bring his car, he said you would be more comfortable.' He paused a moment to adjust the straps of his seat-belt, then continued: 'He is no doubt correct in his assumption—he usually is, unfortunately. It makes arguing with him very difficult. One always has the uncomfortable feeling that even should one win the argument Francisco will be proved right eventually.' He shrugged expressively, 'This is perhaps why people rarely oppose my brother—with the exception of you, of course.' He turned to smile at Liz. 'You are regarded with some awe by all my family. Are you aware of the fact?'

Liz smiled without troubling to reply. She was in the grip of a delicious lethargy. The air-conditioned comfort of the car, combined with Carlos's relaxing company, provided a violent contrast to the riotous colour and the blazing heat of the Andalucian afternoon. She felt as though she was in a cocoon, cushioned at least temporarily from the troubles of the world.

She made an effort to regain her self-control and turned resolutely towards Carlos. 'It would have been pleasant to look around Seville. Do you think I'll be able to come again, later in the week?'

'I shall be happy to escort you ... there is much to see in the area.'

'That's very kind of you,' Liz said with genuine pleasure, fully alert now that they had left the confines of the city. 'However do you manage to grow anything in this baking heat?' she asked, staring out at the shimmering landscape.

'It is true that in many ways it is a hard land to cultivate. To the west and towards the coast are the marshes; towards the east, mountains.' Carlos shrugged his broad shoulders expressively. 'We have to grow the vines in a special way—in pits which are filled with earth and trap the moisture. Our estate is, of course, mainly in the valley of the Guadalquivir, one of the most fertile areas in the whole country. We are very fortunate ... but I will let Francisco tell you about the land, he is more knowledgeable than I am, he has much feeling for his inheritance. ...'

He paused a moment as though uncertain of his next words. 'Your son ... you were able to arrange for someone to care for him?'

'Yes. And he'll spend some time with John Spencer, the man I hope...intend to marry.'

'Of course, it is good that the boy will have a father.'

Carlos seemed unwilling to break the silence during the remainder of the journey and Liz sat quietly, absorbed in her own thoughts; although as they neared their destination her stomach began to feel decidedly uneasy, as even the springs of the Rolls succumbed to the appalling road conditions.

But all thoughts of personal discomfort were driven out of Liz's mind by her first sight of Riera. It shimmered in the torrid landscape, a green oasis smothered in a riot of colour; bougainvillea and other exotic plants growing in wild profusion. Liz gave a gasp of pleasure and sat entranced as Carlos manoeuvred the car expertly into the courtyard.

Her thoughts returned to the present as he braked firmly and switched off the engine. 'Who will be at the house? Is your mother staying at the moment?'

'No, she is still with her sister in Madrid. Don't worry, Liz,' Carlos said with a smile. 'We are not a very over-powering company. Besides Francisco and myself there is only Marisa, our youngest sister. She should be waiting now, I think; she is looking forward to meeting you again.'

'Oh yes, I met her when I visited your parents in Madrid; I remember.' Liz frowned slightly as she tried to remember the details of their last meeting. The truth was that in the early days of their relationship, Francisco's presence had caused everyone else to pale into insignificance. She silently resolved that on this visit personalities would not enter into the situation. It was going to be strictly business. . . .

She smiled in answer to Carlos's questioning glance, 'I don't remember Marisa very clearly, I'm afraid, but in any case she will have changed considerably in the last nine years—she'll be a young lady now.'

'Yes,' Carlos agreed. 'Come along we had better go into the house. You will be cooler there.'

Liz climbed gracefully out of the car as he held the door for her, but her smile of thanks wavered as a tall, masculine figure emerged from the shelter of an outbuilding. Liz was granted a few moments' breathing space in which to school her face into a mask of cool indifference as Carlos greeted his brother in surprise.

'Your business was accomplished more quickly than you expected, Francisco?'

'That is so.' Francisco turned his attention to Liz and gave her a cool bow. 'I regret that I was unable to meet you personally. Carlos explained that I was called away suddenly to deal with a business matter?'

'Yes, thank you—he did explain.' Liz managed to

retain her cool composure and her tone was as formal as Francisco's own, but inwardly she seethed with a mixture of anger and distress. If she had imagined that Francisco had intended her visit to be a friendly one, he had rapidly disabused her of the idea. She felt certain that his manner would have been more welcoming had she been a complete stranger.

She gave herself a mental shake and forced a feeling of anger to smother her distress. Her memory of Francisco's arrogance and lack of sensitivity was obviously not at fault, and her feelings of guilt at dissembling about Edward's parentage began to disappear as her anger grew.

Francisco gestured for her to precede him into the hall and she walked proudly in front of him, her head erect and her eyes sparkling with anger, bright flags of colour burning in her cheeks. She was very conscious of Francisco's gaze on her back and she turned suddenly and raised her brows questioningly as he continued to stare intently at her.

'Is anything wrong?'

'No!' he said abruptly, his cool manner unreadable, but she felt her colour deepen as he continued to scrutinise her from beneath his hooded lids.

He turned away almost impatiently as a plump, dark-haired woman entered the hall. 'Here is Ana, she will show you to your room and serve some refreshments. As you know, we dine late in Spain, so you will have time to rest before dinner.' He paused a moment and then added, 'If you agree I should like to speak to you in my study before we dine. Shall we say nine-thirty?'

Liz realised that once again events were being organised over her head, but Francisco was perfectly correct in his assumptions. She would like to rest, and a light meal in her room sounded wonderful. 'As you wish,' she said, turning to smile her farewell at Carlos, before following the ample form of the housekeeper to her rooms on the first floor.

Her brief glimpse of the house had prepared her for elegance and luxury, and she was not disappointed. Not only had she a bedroom and bathroom but she had also been given a beautifully appointed sitting room, decorated in attractive shades of green, blue and white. All the floors of the suite were tiled uniformly, with cool blue and white terrazzo tiles; and luxurious white rugs were placed casually around the room. The bedroom had the added advantage of a balcony overlooking the inner courtyard, and exotic perfumes from the garden drifted beguilingly into the room.

The main area of the house was planned around the courtyard, and all the rooms on the upper floor had balconies, supported by marble pillars, entwined with bougainvillea and passionflowers and other exotic plants that Liz did not recognise.

As she turned back into the bedroom she saw that one long wall was taken up by a large walk-in wardrobe, and she glanced wryly at her solitary case lying on the cool tiles. Ana had begun to unpack her meagre wardrobe and her few items of clothing hung incongruously on the empty rails.

'I will come and unpack the rest of the Señora's luggage when the cases are delivered from the airport,' Ana said, shaking the folds out of the remaining cotton dress and hanging it in the cupboard.

'I ... er ... I haven't anything else with me. There aren't any other cases,' Liz explained, unable to prevent the faint colour from rising in her cheeks. 'I shall only be here for a few days. . . .'

'Of course, *señora*. . . . Ah, here is some refreshment! Would you like the food in here or in the sitting room?' she asked as a young maid wheeled a loaded trolley into the room.

'Oh, in here, please!' said Liz, looking with increasing longing at the comfortable bed, covered with the crisp white counterpane.

'I will send one of the girls to awaken the Señora in plenty of time for dinner.'

'Thank you. Oh, I almost forgot. I have to see my . . . the Señor before dinner. . . .'

'*Si*, Don Francisco informed me of this. Do not worry— everything is taken care of!'

After the housekeeper left the room Liz ate a little of the delicious food prepared for her and drank two refreshing cups of tea. Then she kicked off her shoes casually, and slowly stripped off the crumpled clothes that she had travelled in, too weary even to hang them in the wardrobe. With a sigh she lowered the immaculate counterpane and crept wearily between the cool silken sheets, slipping almost immediately into a heavy dreamless slumber.

She woke in the perfumed dusk, feeling refreshed and a great deal more ready to face the ordeal of a meeting alone with Francisco. There was a tray beside the bed containing a fresh pot of tea, and the sound of water running in the adjoining bathroom.

Ana's face appeared around the door. 'Ah, you are awake! Your bath will be ready as soon as you have finished your tea. Shall I lay out your clothes for the evening?'

'Oh no, that won't be necessary, thank you. And thank you for the tea, Ana . . . it's delicious,' Liz added, cautiously sipping the steaming liquid.

'It is a pleasure, *señora*,' Ana beamed. 'I shall return later and take you to Don Francisco,' she said, before leaving the room.

Liz lay quietly for a long moment after the housekeeper had left, luxuriating in the unaccustomed luxury of her surroundings. Then with a deliberate effort she slid out of the bed and carried her towelling robe into the steamy bathroom. Ana had laced the water liberally with expensively perfumed bathsalts and Liz lazed for a few minutes in the water, fruitlessly contemplating the contents of her wardrobe. Her choice for the evening would not be an overwhelmingly difficult one. It would probably have to be the long blue and white shirt-waister. It was not exactly haute couture, but it did have the virtue of emphasising her fair colouring and slim figure.

Lovingly she remembered the expensive wardrobe of evening clothes that she had left in the London flat nine years ago. Of course they would have been totally unsuitable for her life-style in the intervening years, she smiled a little wryly to herself. Jeans and sweaters were far more suitable for bringing up children than mink and diamonds.

Eventually she stepped out of the bath on to the fluffy mat, drying her scented skin until it tingled and glowed. She opened the capacious wardrobe and extracted the simple dress, laying it carefully on the bed until she had completed her make-up, winding her hair into the familiar knot and applying her eye make-up carefully. Grey shadow to give depth to her warm blue eyes and a skilled application of dark mascara. She stared at her reflection in the mirror and was forced to admit that she was lucky to have such a good skin. Creamy and smooth, it needed no adornment.

She reached into her bag for her lipstick and coloured her mouth skilfully, outlining it first with lip pencil and finishing with a light application of gloss. Finally she slipped into the shirtwaister, fastening the buttons with hands that trembled slightly. The reflection that gazed at her from the mirror was a reassuring one. She looked elegant and composed, the perfect complement to Don Francisco Ramirez de Riera, but inwardly she was a seething mass of nerves as she thought of the coming interview.

Her disruptive thoughts were interrupted by a soft tapping on the panelling of the door and Ana entered in response to her invitation.

'Ah, *señora*! Don Francisco asked me to see if you were ready.'

'Yes . . . yes, I am.'

'If you would come this way, please. The Señor is waiting.'

Liz followed Ana's ample form down the stairs and into the spacious hall, breathing slowly and deeply in an effort to regain her composure. Francisco's study led directly out of the large, tiled hall, and as Ana knocked on the imposing wooden door, Liz schooled her features into a mask of calm indifference.

Ana opened the door and Liz found herself in a softly lighted room, with Francisco leaning indolently against the wall gazing out of large french windows into the inner courtyard. He turned and moved away from the windows as she entered the room, and Liz forced herself to remain unperturbed as his coldly indifferent gaze swept over her. Her first thought was that his appearance was as immaculate as it had always been, his evening suit a model of restrained good taste, the severe white lines of his shirt providing a startling contrast to his swarthy, dark-browed countenance.

'Please be seated,' he said abruptly, indicating a chair to one side of the highly polished desk. 'I shall not keep you long. There are a few matters that I wish to discuss with you . . . things that I should like you to consider during your stay here,' he added, his hard gaze continuing to survey her arrogantly.

Under the challenge of his appraisal her body stiffened and she raised her chin defiantly, determined not to be browbeaten by his insufferable attitude.

'I can't believe that we really have anything to discuss after all these years, Francisco.' Her voice was deliberately cool and she had the dubious satisfaction of seeing his mouth tighten in response to her deliberate provocation. She felt a faint stirring of excitement as she realised that she could still penetrate some of the defences of this self-controlled stranger.

'I want you to withdraw your petition for divorce,' Francisco said abruptly, and as Liz would have interrupted he continued, 'One moment, please, let me explain further before you begin to protest. You need not fear that I have any plans to resume a more personal relationship with you. ... I have little interest in you as a woman. Any desire that I may have felt for you faded many years ago, you can be assured of that.' He stared at her with barely concealed dislike and added almost contemptuously: 'The thought of a divorce does not please me; there has never been one in the family and I do not intend to change this tradition.'

'But surely you want children ... I mean. ...'

He glared accusingly at her. 'As you say, I would have liked a son of my own ... however, that is unlikely in the circumstances. Carlos will be my heir. He will marry and have sons to carry on the name. You are my wife in the sight of God, Lizbeth, and I intend that you shall remain so! There will be a generous financial arrangement made, of course. Your life will be a great deal more comfortable than it is at the present time,' he added with supreme arrogance.

It was clear that Francisco did not expect any opposition to his plans, and Liz fumed inwardly, but managed to maintain an outward appearance of composure as she said: 'I'm afraid you've wasted my time and your money if this is the only reason you asked me here. I haven't the slightest intention of withdrawing my application for a divorce. If you choose to cling to this ... this ... apology for a marriage there is, of course, no reason why you should remarry, but I intend to do so as soon as the divorce is finalised. Now, if you'll excuse me. ...'

She rose quickly and began to move towards the door, but Francisco reached it before her and leaned heavily against the panelling, preventing any further move on her part.

'I think not,' he drawled in deceptively quiet tones. 'We have not finished our ... discussion.' He paused a moment to regard her cynically. 'I confess that you have surprised me. I was unaware that you were planning to remarry. I am obviously not as well informed as I had thought.'

Liz made a tremendous effort to regain her self-control and forced herself to return his raking glance. 'It must surely have been obvious to you that I wanted a divorce so that I could remarry. There would have been little point in bothering after all these years without such a reason.'

'It is true that when you first refused to come to Spain I wondered whether you had managed to snare another wealthy fool.'

Liz's lips tightened in anger and she made an involuntary move towards the door, but Francisco merely smiled mockingly and made no attempt to allow her to pass.

'Carlos assured me that you had not the appearance of a woman kept by a wealthy man,' he continued, as though there had been no interruption. 'But it would appear that he was mistaken. As a matter of interest, why did you not marry Mellor after we parted? You bore his child, did you not?' he said with scarcely veiled contempt. 'Did your attractions not survive closer appraisal, hmm? Or were his monetary assets not sufficient for you? You have perhaps been playing for higher game?'

Francisco's manner was as smooth as silk, but Liz was not deceived. She trembled inwardly as she sensed the unleashed violence in the man, like a panther waiting to spring. She had experienced his anger in the past and had no wish to do so again, but his last words were a goad to her pride.

'How dare you speak to me in that fashion? You ignorant, unfeeling man! Let me out of this room at once—do you hear me?' She was almost beside herself with rage and felt no fear even when he began to move menacingly towards her.

However, her instinct for self-preservation was still active, and involuntarily she stepped away from him, a realisation of her own vulnerability coming to her rather belatedly.

'Let me go, Francisco! Please, let me go!' she said, her voice husky with some undefined emotion. 'You have no right to keep me here. . . .'

'No right? My beautiful cheat of a wife, I assure you that I have every right to do exactly as I wish with you. Do you understand me?' He reached forward and gripped her upper arms, drawing her relentlessly towards him. 'Perhaps I should demonstrate my rights to you,' he said harshly. 'Would you like that, my dear wife? Shall I perhaps father my heir now? Would you like to bear a child to your loving husband?'

As he spoke Francisco thrust his face close to Liz's, his mouth twisted with anger and his eyes flaming with suppressed emotion. Liz gazed at him with wide, pleading eyes, but for a moment it seemed that he intended to carry out his threat. He drew her inexorably closer to him until she could feel the masculine strength of his body and hear the wild beating of his heart above her own.

For a long moment he gazed at her vulnerable mouth, an unreadable expression in his eyes, and Liz felt her body melting in his embrace. She knew that if he chose to enforce his will she would be unable to prevent him; and she was forced to admit to herself that she wanted nothing more than to feel that sensual mouth devouring her own and those once familiar hands caressing her body. . . .

'Please, Francisco,' she whispered in undesignedly provocative tones, her lips parting under his gaze in unconscious invitation.

'*Madre de Dios*, Lizbeth!' he groaned, pushing her forcibly away, and a wealth of conflicting emotions raced through Lizbeth's brain. Dear God, what a fool she had been! She ought never to have come to Spain; John had been right. She shivered inwardly as she realised that she had invited Francisco's attentions.

With one last, desperate look at Francisco's stiff, unyielding figure staring broodingly out of the window, she fled without hindrance into the hall, and began to climb the stairs on trembling legs, barely conscious of the tears coursing down her cheeks, only intent upon gaining the privacy of her room.

She awoke to the sound of blinds being drawn, and sat up hastily in bed, only to struggle down again with a suppressed exclamation as she realised that beneath the silken sheets she was completely naked. She had no recollection of undressing or getting into bed the previous evening, but gradually her memory returned and a feeling of impending disaster began to grow, so that she found it difficult to respond adequately to Ana's cheerful greeting.

The older woman came to the side of the bed, her face marred by a worried frown. 'I have woken you too early, señora? I am sorry! I will take away the tray and draw the blinds—you will sleep again?' she added anxiously.

'No, no! There's no need, Ana. I'm perfectly okay,' Liz said reassuringly. 'For a moment I didn't remember where I was. I . . . er . . . I'm afraid I missed dinner yesterday,' she added. 'Was everyone annoyed . . .?'

'But no, señora! The Señor, he explained that you were tired, and had already fallen asleep. I came in later to see whether you would like a meal in your room, but you were still asleep. I have brought rolls and preserves now—I think maybe you are very hungry?'

'Yes . . . yes! Thank you, Ana. That was a very kind thought.' Liz reached for the robe at the side of her bed and slipped her feet on to the cool tiles with the intention of freshening up a little before eating the food that Ana had provided.

When she returned to the bedroom the housekeeper

had left. It must have been Ana who had put her to bed the previous evening, she thought thankfully; she had certainly slept heavily.

As she poured herself a cup of coffee she glanced casually at the travelling alarm clock on the bedside table and almost dropped the coffee pot on to the floor. It was ten past twelve! Hazy, half-formed plans for returning to England would have to be abandoned for today; it was highly unlikely that she would be able to arrange transport at this late hour.

She groaned and threw herself backwards on the luxuriously appointed bed, pulling the silken sheets over her head in an attempt to shut out unpalatable realities.

Her thoughts returned to the evening before and she was forced to admit that there was no doubt about the fact that she was still physically attracted to Francisco. No other man had ever been able to turn her limbs to water in quite such a way. She shivered inwardly. Not even John had that effect on her, but she must not forget for a moment that their love was built on a solid foundation of mutual trust, not on infatuation or lust, and every extra moment spent in Francisco's house put that trust and their future together in jeopardy.

She would have to speak to Francisco at lunch, she determined with a sigh, and ask him to arrange for her to be taken back to Seville. After all, he could hardly keep her here against her will, could he?

With her plan of action decided she became aware of the distinctly empty feeling in her stomach, and drawing the tray which Ana had provided on to her knees, she devoured the fresh, crisp rolls hungrily. The coffee was refreshing and fragrant and when she finally climbed out of bed she was considerably more cheerful.

She ran the shower bracingly cool, and with drops of water still trickling over her slim body she opened the capacious wardrobe and extracted a pair of white cotton pants and a glowing red halter-necked top.

In a moment of bravado she decided to wear the top without a bra. Francisco would disapprove, of course, that was only be expected, but she hated worrying about straps showing, and her breasts were still young and firm. It was a stupid convention anyway, she decided recklessly. After a moment's deliberation she left her hair swinging loosely around her shoulders and slipping her feet into a pair of high-heeled leather mules she felt ready to face the day.

She discovered that although the house was large, the simple design made it easy to find her way about, and she was soon standing once again in the cool tiled hall. She hesitated a moment, wondering whether to try one of the closed wooden doors leading out of the hall, or whether to go into the garden, when the door of a small room on her right opened and a girl emerged.

She was slim and young with rather demure, old-fashioned clothing, which nevertheless could not detract from the pure, clear-skinned beauty of her face.

The girl smiled shyly and Liz responded warmly to her. 'Hello! You must be Marisa. I'm Liz,' she said, holding out her hand and having it firmly shaken.

'Yes, I am Marisa. I am pleased to meet you, Liz. I hope you are feeling better this morning?' she asked quietly. 'We were a little worried about you yesterday evening. Francisco said that the journey had tired you— he explained that you were not fond of flying. I hate flying myself,' Marisa added with an understanding smile, 'it always makes me feel very sick.' She grimaced with remembered distaste, and Liz laughed softly.

'Please—what am I thinking of? Come and sit down. Lunch will not be ready for ten minutes or so, we have time to talk a little,' said Marisa, leading Liz into the small sitting room from which she had just emerged.

It was a comfortable room, with well worn chairs, a hi-fi and a large selection of records. The shelves were packed with paperbacks in a higgledy-piggledy fashion, and Liz was not surprised to learn that it was where the family relaxed when they were alone, although she found it difficult to reconcile her memories of Francisco with this happy clutter. He had always objected to her leaving any books around in the flat when they were first married.

'You do not mind sitting here?' Marisa said apologetically. 'It is not elegant. . . .'

'I don't mind at all,' said Liz with a smile, as she sank on to a chair. 'It reminds me of home, only not quite as untidy.'

'I do not know much about England,' Marisa confessed, 'but you live in the North, do you not? It is very cold and it rains much of the time, is that so?' she asked in slightly puzzled tones.

Liz grinned. 'You can't imagine why anyone should want to live there! It's all those things and more,' she added with a laugh. 'Sometimes it snows for days on end in winter, and even in summer the weather is not reliable. But also it's very beautiful. The fields are green and in spring and summer are filled with wild flowers. There are moors and woodlands and almost every valley has its stream or river. Right now everything is a little drab and dusty, but within a few weeks the leaves will be turning colour. . . . I'm so sorry, am I boring you?' Liz queried, laughing apologetically.

'But no! I am interested,' Marisa interposed. 'Francisco does not talk much about England. Do you live in a town, or is your house remote like the estate?'

Liz laughed. 'No, no, it's absolutely nothing like this! Oh, don't get me wrong,' she interposed hastily, 'this is the most gorgeous house I've ever seen, but,' she shrugged expressively, 'very few people can afford to live this way at home. Look—are you sure you really want to hear all this, or are you just being polite? I mean, I don't want to bore you,' she said uncertainly.

'Please—I am interested,' Marisa said quickly. 'I do not travel very frequently. In Spain the women are closely protected, as you know,' she said a little wistfully. 'I would like to hear.'

'We-ell, I live in a small village on the side of a valley. The town where I work is in the valley bottom and the hillsides around are dotted with small villages and poor farms. I live in a terraced house—that's a row of houses all joined together to save space,' Liz explained. 'They're tucked into the side of the hill, so are quite small, but we have a living room and a large kitchen that we eat our meals in, two bedrooms and a bathroom. Oh, and we have a small front garden and a garage at the back of the house. The back garden is surprisingly big; it was very useful for Edward to play in when he was younger,' she said carelessly, only to give herself a mental shake as she saw the embarrassment on Marisa's face.

Fortunately at that moment there was a tap on the door and Ana entered to announce that lunch was ready, and both Liz and Marisa were only too pleased to follow the housekeeper into a small dining room farther down the hall.

Liz had little time to prepare herself for a meeting with Francisco, but in the event she had no need to worry. The table was set with only two places, but her relief was shortlived as she realised that her request for transport back to Seville would have to be delayed once again.

She sighed inwardly but forced herself to compliment Marisa upon their attractive surroundings. French doors opened into the inner courtyard and a bewildering variety of plants had been brought inside in large tubs and pots, so that the room appeared to be a continuation of the garden.

Ana made sure that both girls were comfortable and then proceeded to serve large bowls of gazpacho, with more of her light and crispy home-made rolls. For some minutes there was silence in the room as both Marisa and Liz did justice to Ana's cooking. It was Marisa who spoke first. 'Edward is your son, I think?'

'Yes. I'm sorry if I embarrassed you by mentioning him.' Liz shrugged expressively, and continued, 'He is such an important part of my life that it's difficult to talk about home without mentioning him.'

'He must be quite old now?'

'Yes. Yes, he has just recently had his eighth birthday. Which reminds me, I must telephone home some time today. He'll be worried.'

'I will take you to Francisco's office after lunch. You may telephone from there,' Marisa told her.

'I think it had better wait until later,' said Liz, putting down her spoon with a sigh of pleasure and wiping her mouth on the king-size linen napkin provided. 'He and John will probably have gone out for the day.'

'You have two sons?' Marisa exclaimed in slightly shocked tones.

'No, no,' Liz said hastily. 'Look, Marisa,' she added after a moment's pause, 'I don't know how much Francisco has told you, but ... well, John is the man I intend to marry. That's why I've asked Francisco for a divorce. Edward is staying with my neighbour, Mrs Helliwell, while I'm in Spain, but John has promised to help to entertain him. He's on holiday from his job as a teacher at the moment and he and Edward normally see a lot of each other. ...'

'I see,' Marisa said quietly. 'Francisco had not said. ... He is very fortunate, this John,' she added, regarding Liz steadily for a moment with her clear young gaze.

Liz felt the warm colour rush into her cheeks at this unexpected compliment, but she was saved from the need to reply by Ana's bustling entrance.

'The soup was delicious, thank you, Ana,' Liz said sincerely.

'I am glad you enjoyed it, *señora*. Now there is only an omelette with salad and then fresh fruit but I can bring out pastries if you wish?'

'Oh no, the salad and fruit sound lovely,' Liz said with

a smile. 'I don't normally have time to eat much at lunch time, just coffee and a sandwich in between work and dashing to the shops.'

'That is why you have no flesh on your bones,' Ana sniffed in disgust. 'Now that you are here I shall see that you eat properly.' She placed a large, fluffy omelette in front of Liz and said, 'Eat plenty of salad too, it is good for you. You hear, Señorita Marisa?'

Marisa grinned as the housekeeper left the room and explained:

'Ana cannot understand why neither myself, Francisco or Carlos put on weight. We are a great disappointment to her, I am afraid. She will be turning all her efforts towards you while you are staying with us,' Marisa added, piling a large helping of salad on to her plate.

'I'd be as fat as a pig if I stayed here any length of time,' Liz said with a laugh, as she savoured the delicious melt-in-the-mouth omelette. 'But . . . well, I shan't be here long enough. In fact I was hoping that Francisco would be at lunch, I wanted him to arrange for me to go home today, if that's possible,' she said firmly, deliberately ignoring the look of dismay on the younger girl's face.

'But you were to stay a week,' Marisa protested. 'Francisco told us last evening that you may even stay longer.'

'I don't know what can have given Francisco that idea,' Liz said, determinedly banishing the all too vivid memory of their last moments together in the study.

'I don't want to seem rude—I would have liked to stay and get to know you better—but after speaking to Francisco yesterday it's obvious that I can't do as he wishes. I would be staying under false pretences if I said otherwise.' She shrugged wearily, mentally cursing Francisco for putting her in the difficult position.

'I do not think that Francisco will be home until much later, and then there is to be a dinner party this evening. Ana will have prepared. . . .'

'It looks as though I shall have to stay until tomorrow then, doesn't it? Oh, I'm sorry, Marisa,' Liz added as she saw the younger girl's expression. 'I know it isn't your fault. It's just that the whole situation is so ridiculous. I must have been mad to come in the first place!'

After a moment her sense of proportion reasserted itself and she gave a reluctant grin. 'Do you think you can put up with me for the rest of the day, or not? Now you know why Francisco and I split up,' she said drily. 'We are too much alike!'

'I had thought that perhaps you would like to look around the house and gardens after lunch, and then perhaps a swim,' Marisa said hesitantly.

'That sounds terrific! I didn't know you had a pool!'

'Yes. Francisco had it built a few years ago after our father died.'

Although Liz was still worried about her ambiguous position in the household she managed to do full justice to Ana's cooking and after refusing a third of the delicious home-grown peaches she sighed luxuriously and, pushing back her chair, followed Marisa into the inner courtyard where the housekeeper had set the coffee on a small wrought iron table beside one of the supporting pillars.

'This really is the most beautiful place. I could become addicted to it very quickly,' she added, settling into a comfortable lounger and taking the coffee that Marisa provided. 'Is it always so pleasant ... even in the colder weather?'

'But yes! To me it is always home, much more so than the house in Madrid. Did Francisco not bring you here when you came to Spain with him?' Marisa asked tentatively.

'No. We stayed in Madrid and its environs during that visit. All this,' she gave an encompassing gesture, 'was to be a surprise for later, when we were free to spend plenty of time here ... I must admit that I was partly to blame for our not visiting,' Liz said with a shrug. 'Francisco wanted to spend part of our honeymoon here, but after my last meeting with your parents I am afraid I was not very enthusiastic. I am just a coward at heart,' she added with a wry smile.

'Look, why don't we change the subject and talk about you? What are you going to do when you leave the convent school?' Liz asked, turning to the other girl enquiringly.

'I am to stay at school for another year. I enjoy studying and Francisco is willing,' Marisa added quietly. 'And then—who knows? It has been understood for some time that I would marry Juan Diego. He is a neighbour, you understand—our families have been friends for many years.'

'This boy Juan, do you love him?' Liz interposed quietly.

'We have always got on well together. As to love . . . I do not know,' Marisa said slowly.

'I see! And if you decided that you didn't want to marry the boy, what would happen?'

'I have never thought about the possibility,' Marisa replied. 'Juan is happy with the arrangement, and I too have agreed. . . .'

'Is there nothing that you would like to do first?' Liz queried. 'Before you marry and start a family, I mean.'

Marisa hesitated a moment and then said quietly, 'I have often thought that I should like to go to university and learn more about the history of my country. What the stones and remains of old buildings can tell us.'

'You mean archaeology?' Liz asked.

'Yes! But it is not to be, and I am quite happy to marry Juan. He says that we will build a small house on his father's estate and live there until he inherits. It will be the kind of life that I am familiar with. . . .'

'Have you mentioned the university idea to Francisco . . . or your mother?' Liz asked.

'No! Oh no!' Marisa protested in alarmed tones. 'They

would not approve. It would cause them distress . . . and
it is after all only a foolish dream. Please,' she added
urgently, 'you will not speak of this!'

'Calm down!' said Liz with a laugh. 'I was interested
that's all. I'm not in the habit of giving secrets away.
Look, if you've finished your coffee why don't we go for
that sightseeing tour? Perhaps we can cool off in the pool
later?'

CHAPTER FIVE

Ten minutes later the girls were walking companionably away from the house towards the small stable block. Liz had borrowed a rather striking wide-brimmed Cordoban hat from Marisa; and, at the younger girl's tentative suggestion, had covered her unprotected arms and shoulders with a cream cheesecloth shirt, which hung loosely outside her trousers.

Liz had been unprepared for the harsh brilliance of the early afternoon sun and she thought longingly of the sunglasses she had left in her bedroom, as she screwed up her eyes against the sun's glare. It was now that she saw the need for the inner courtyard of the house; with its cool fountain and lush green foliage it provided a splendid retreat from the overpowering midday heat.

'Don't you usually have a siesta at this time, Marisa? I thought it was only mad dogs and Englishmen who ventured out in the midday sun.'

'*Si*-sometimes we rest in our rooms or by the pool. I think we should go for a swim soon,' said Marisa, with a glance in Lizbeth's direction. 'You will become very tired if you walk in this unaccustomed heat for too long. Here are the horses,' she added, leading Liz into a small self-contained courtyard surrounded by store-rooms and horseboxes, with their sleek, well groomed occupants regarding the two newcomers with interest.

'These are the horses which we ride regularly,' Marisa explained. 'If you stay longer I will take you riding—we will explore a little of the surrounding countryside.'

'I would have enjoyed that,' said Liz, 'but in any case my riding is a little rusty, I'm afraid. I don't get the opportunity to ride . . . we haven't either the time or money

78

for me to indulge,' she explained, in answer to Marisa's look of enquiry.

'I expect you would quickly acquire the skill again.'

'Perhaps so,' said Liz in noncommittal tones. 'Doesn't Francisco breed horses? Were these horses bred here?'

'On the *estancia*, yes, but not here. We have a large stud farther down the valley. It is Francisco's great pride and joy; I will take you later in the week . . . if you are still here,' Marisa added quietly. 'Come, meet some of the horses and then we will continue our tour.'

The next half hour passed swiftly, with an easy camaraderie quickly developing between Liz and Marisa. Liz discovered that Marisa had a warm and gentle nature with the added advantage of a lively sense of humour, and she was unable to resist comparing her personality with that of Francisco.

'You are not very like Francisco in temperament, are you, Marisa? Although from your appearance no one could doubt your relationship.'

Marisa paused a moment before replying as though choosing her words with care. 'It is true that we are different in many ways, although it is not always easy to tell . . . I am not subject to the same tremendous pressures as Francisco. He has many business worries and great responsibilities. I cannot tell how I would respond to similar circumstances.' She shrugged and continued, 'In some ways we are very alike. We are both very possessive with those we love; it is a bad fault, I think, and can create many problems and much misunderstanding. But it is because we do not give our love carelessly, and then we love, perhaps too deeply. I think it makes us demand more than most people are willing to give. I am sorry,' she added, after shooting a glance at Liz's averted face, 'I am afraid another of my faults is to speak when perhaps I should not. That was not very tactful, I think.'

'Don't worry, Marisa,' Liz said quietly, gazing moodily at the ground and idly kicking a stray pebble across the courtyard. 'You are probably correct in your assessment of the situation. Our marriage never really had a fighting chance. I was far too young and foolish to have married in the first place, and Francisco was ... well, I don't really think I want to continue this conversation; and I'm sure that Francisco would not approve the direction it's taking. How about that swim you promised me? I'm beginning to feel rather like a wet dishcloth!' she added with a grin.

'You do not look anything like a ... wet dishcloth,' Marisa replied, stumbling over the unfamiliar words, 'but I think you are right, it is time we went for a swim, if only so that Diego and Jaime can begin work again,' she said with a quiet smile, indicating the two stable boys outside the tack room, watching Liz with scarcely veiled appreciation. 'They have been staring at you with their mouths open for the last fifteen minutes, and Francisco would definitely not approve,' she added, steering Liz in the direction of the house.

The pool was large and luxurious, with a beautiful summerhouse and patio where loungers were placed, and it was surrounded by lush, palm-fringed gardens. Fortunately Liz had brought her bikini with her, and she was pleased that she had done so when she saw Marisa's demure, old-fashioned costume. It was clear that the younger girl would not have had anything suitable to lend to her.

In truth, although the bikini had seemed quite decent on holiday last year and even at the local lido, when compared to Marisa Liz felt decidedly underdressed. The blue bikini clung lovingly to her pale, creamy body. The halter neckline emphasised her full breasts, but the briefs were skimpy enough to show that she had not gained any unnecessary weight in the last few years.

Marisa stared at the costume with a mixture of shock and envy which increased Liz's discomfort, so that she slid hastily into the cool depths of the pool and began to swim, the full length energetically. Before she had gained the halfway mark she was overtaken by Marisa's sleek body, which was obviously completely at home in the water.

'You must swim regularly,' Liz remarked, gasping after her brief exertion, as Marisa floated idly on her back in the warm, shallow water.

'*Si*, we all enjoy swimming. Francisco has little time for other sports, with his many business interests, and he taught me to swim many years ago.'

'He was always a strong swimmer,' Liz murmured quietly, remembering their honeymoon in Barbados, and how she had enjoyed watching Francisco's sleek, muscular body cutting through the water.... She gave herself a mental shake; the pleasanter memories of their life together were coming all too often to her mind since she had arrived in Spain.

Determinedly she climbed from the pool and stretched her length on one of the comfortable loungers, placing a pair of sunglasses firmly on her nose.

'I'm going to sunbathe for a time,' she called.

'But of course,' Marisa replied, climbing quickly out of the pool and placing her dripping body beside Liz's supine form. 'You must make sure that you are well covered with oil and do not stay too long in the sun—your skin will burn quickly,' she warned. 'Me, I cannot understand why fair people should wish to sunbathe. In our country a pale skin is much admired. I have always longed for a pale complexion,' she added with a derisive gesture at her own perfect olive features.

'Mm, the ways of the world are strange,' Liz murmured lazily, taking the sun oil which Marisa handed to her and carefully smoothing it over her body.

When she had finished, Marisa applied a little to her already warmly tanned skin and lay down beside her guest. They were interrupted briefly by Ana bringing cold drinks, and shortly afterwards Liz moved her lounger into the shade of the summerhouse, as she had no wish to appear at dinner an unbecoming shade of scarlet.

Marisa also moved into the summerhouse, and both girls lazed companionably until Liz began to have the uneasy feeling that they were being watched. She raised herself on one arm and gazed into the nearby gardens without discovering anyone, and as Marisa seemed undisturbed she forced herself to ignore the tingling sensation along her spine. Eventually the feeling became so strong that she felt compelled to rise uncertainly and hurry down to the pool, sliding ignominiously into the cool water, ashamed of her own fears. Immediately she felt better and began swimming in a leisurely fashion around the pool.

Suddenly her mouth and eyes were filled with water as a figure dived close behind her into the pool. Coughing and spluttering noisily, she waited for Marisa to surface in order to gain her revenge, only to find herself gazing into Francisco's dark, unreadable features.

'Oh! I . . . I thought you were Marisa,' Liz gasped in shocked tones.

'Had you known that it was I you would not have waited so patiently for me to surface, eh? Is that not so?' Francisco said in harsh tones. 'Oh, do not worry, Lizbeth, I shall not disturb you,' he added, turning abruptly away and beginning to swim powerfully down the side of the pool.

Unwillingly aware that he had already disturbed her far too much for her peace of mind, Liz breathed deeply, endeavouring to quieten the rapid beating of her heart and put out of her mind any thoughts of the heavily muscled figure forging his way powerfully down the pool.

She almost welcomed being submerged once more by a huge splash as Marisa surfaced, spluttering and laughing, beside her.

'If anyone else does that . . .' said Liz, raising her fist

threateningly at the younger girl.

'I am sorry, Liz, I just could not resist it,' Marisa said with an apologetic laugh. 'Come on, I will race you for two lengths—si? I will give you a start to make it more equal.'

'Okay,' Liz sighed in resigned tones. 'And I thought this was going to be a life of ease and luxury! Here am I, almost drowned on two occasions forced to swim races against an Olympic champion.'

'Not so,' Marisa replied with a laugh. 'If you exert yourself it may be that you will beat me.'

Liz, of course, finished well behind Marisa, and she was lazily treading water in the centre of the pool, being instructed by an earnest Marisa in ways to improve her swimming speed, when suddenly the girl disappeared with startling rapidity beneath the surface, only to emerge once more some distance away, held at arm's length from Francisco's muscular chest, as she attempted to free herself laughingly from his grasp.

'So, my little sister pretends that you could beat her in a swimming race, does she?' he said in mock-serious tones, holding Marisa's wrists firmly in one hand and pulling her towards Liz. 'She is able to beat both Carlos and myself with ease. I think I shall have to give her a little more of the same punishment,' he added with a wicked grin, as Marisa began to protest laughingly and struggle fiercely in his grasp.

Before Liz had time to come to terms with the rapid alteration in Francisco's mood, both he and his sister disappeared once again from view; and Liz peered into the rippling blue depths in an attempt to discern their figures.

She had only enough time to take a quick gulp of air before she in her turn felt her ankle firmly grasped and she was pulled inexorably beneath the surface. She had never mastered the art of opening her eyes beneath the water without a mask. But she was in no doubt as to the owner of the arms which grasped her tightly around the waist and drew her struggling body close to his.

Abruptly they began to rise, and as they broke surface she opened her eyes, only to close them again involuntarily, as she encountered an expression of naked desire upon Francisco's face. She knew that she ought to be struggling—ought at least to attempt to make him release her—but instead her limbs seemed to melt completely against his hard, demanding body.

Again she drew a trembling breath as she felt him beginning to pull her under the water; and as they moved sinuously beneath the surface only one coherent thought emerged from the confusion in her brain. It was a vivid memory of Francisco's words at their last meeting; his denial of any feelings of desire for her.

His last unguarded look flashed across her brain and she knew that whatever else he felt for her, his desire was as strong as ever, and every moment that their embrace continued Liz knew that her own powers of resistance were weakened. Their bodies had forgotten the last nine years' separation and were attempting to merge again into one, and all her anger against Francisco was melting away with startling rapidity. She felt only a growing desire to stay in his arms; to invite his lovemaking. . . .

As they rose again out of the water, Liz summoned every ounce of will power and energy and pushed against Francisco's chest with her hands. As he fell back, momentarily off balance, she swam to the side and scrambled urgently out of the pool.

She glanced back for a moment, seeing the laughter frozen on Marisa's face, as she glanced from Liz to Francisco's angry figure in the water. Then she turned and ran towards the house, snatching up the wrap which Marisa had provided and throwing it quickly over her bikini.

When she reached the sancturary of her room she ran the shower as cold as possible and stood, gasping, beneath its icy shock. Gradually the relentless pounding of the cold water began to bring her to her senses and turning off the shower she began to dry herself briskly. She dared not allow herself time to relax, the traitorous impulses of her own body every time she came into contact with Francisco had made her more determined than ever to leave Spain at the earliest possible opportunity.

Involuntarily she sighed. Edward would have to manage without his riding lessons after all, as she could certainly never accept any money from Francisco in the present circumstances. In fact, for the sake of her own peace of mind she must never see or communicate with Francisco again, she thought fiercely, her anger against him growing, now that she was away from his dominating presence. He quite obviously despised her and yet seemed to think he could indulge his desires for her as though she was his mistress!

. Hurriedly she dressed again in trousers and sun-top, drying her hair swiftly with the dryer provided. She would telephone Edward and John immediately, she decided. It would be a relief to hear their voices again and they would be getting worried about her. . . .

Hastily she gave her hair a final brush and slipping a pair of sandals on to her feet, she hurried from the room. In all likelihood Francisco and Marisa would still be in the pool, she thought hopefully, and Ana would be able to show her the phone.

The housekeeper was putting the finishing touches to an elegant flower arrangement in the hall as Liz came down the stairs, and she was pleased at Liz's involuntary exclamation of pleasure when she saw the design.

'I am pleased that you like it, *señora*,' she said. 'Always I do special arrangements when we are to have guests.' She gave a characteristic shrug, 'My girls are no good at these things! Now, how can I help you, *señora*? Don Francisco is still in the garden if you wish to speak with him.'

'No! Oh no!' Liz demurred hastily. 'I was wondering whether I could use the telephone—I . . . er . . . I want to phone home—to England,' she explained tentatively.

'But of course, *señora*! I will show you the telephone in Don Francisco's study.'

'Oh no—please! I mean . . . look, isn't there a phone elsewhere that I could use? I don't want to be a nuisance,' Liz added lamely.

Ana shot her a puzzled glance. 'Oh, but it is no trouble,' she said reassuringly. 'The Señor is not using the study. Come this way,' she added, leading Liz towards the room in which she had spoken to Francisco the previous evening.

'So, I will leave you now,' she said, opening the door and standing to one side. 'You have everything else that you require?'

'Yes! Yes, thank you, Ana.' Liz smiled at the housekeeper and walked into the room, closing the door behind Ana's departing back.

For a moment she stood with her back against the door, staring at her surroundings. There were a number of large leather armchairs in the room, one of them a huge recliner with a footstool, which Liz felt an immediate urge to sample. The rest of the pieces were highly polished antiques and around three walls there were shelves of leather-bound books which beckoned enticingly to her.

Taking herself firmly in hand, she lifted the telephone and asked tentatively for John's number. It took some time before she was able to make the operator understand; but eventually the girl agreed to make the connection and said she would ring back when she had done so.

Liz was momentarily at a loss when she had replaced the telephone on to its cradle. It was not part of her plans to linger in Francisco's study. She supposed she could go and wait in the living room or the hall, but it would seem a strange thing to do. . . .

In the event her speculation was unnecessary, because

the door opened and Francisco himself walked into the room. For a moment he stood quietly, staring at her, a guarded expression on his dark-browed face. Even in an unexpected pair of jeans, with his shirt opened to the waist revealing his darkly tanned chest, he was a personality to be reckoned with, and Liz felt an increasingly familiar warmth invading her body. Becoming colour suffused her cheeks and her lower limbs began to tremble uncontrollably, so that she leaned heavily against the side of his desk for support.

'You wanted to see me, Lizbeth?' he said, his gaze becoming more intense as it lingered for a moment on the outline of her breasts beneath the sun-top.

Liz gave an inward groan as she realised that she had omitted once more to wear a bra. He would think that she had deliberately entered his study in a state of semi-undress to encourage his attentions. Almost as though he could read her thoughts, he began to move slowly towards her.

'The phone!' Liz gasped in a strangled voice, as the ringing tones cut through the silence that had fallen. 'I came to use the phone,' she said again, attempting to steady her legs and making an undignified lunge in the direction of the offending object as Francisco lifted it lazily to his ear.

'It would seem that your call is available now,' he said after a moment, making no attempt to move away from the desk, and Liz had perforce to stand close beside him as she took the phone from his grasp.

'Hello! Hello, is that you, John?' she said as firmly as she could, when so overwhelmingly aware of the silent figure beside her. She had a disconcertingly direct view of his tanned chest and the urge to reach out and touch him became almost unbearable.

Unconsciously she raised her eyes to his face and gave a startled gasp as she saw the expression in his own. Abruptly she turned her back on his intrusive figure, aware that her voice held a distinct tremble as she replied to John's first greeting.

'Hello, John! It's Liz here. How are you both getting on?' she asked in as steady a tone as she could muster, suddenly filled with an overwhelming longing to be with Edward again.

'We're both fine, love,' John answered. 'But I'm afraid you can't speak to Edward at the moment. . . .'

'Wait—let me guess,' Liz interposed with a choking laugh. 'He's out somewhere playing football, have I guessed correctly?'

'Right first time,' said John with a grin in his voice, 'and no doubt covered in mud from top to toe.'

'Poor John! Is it very bad?'

'No, no, actually I'm enjoying it,' he replied. 'But it would be even better if you were here. When are you coming home, Liz? We're both missing you.'

'Me too, John. Look, it's a bit difficult to talk at the moment, I'm not on my own. Wait a minute,' she added hastily, turning to face Francisco's silent figure. 'I would like to conduct a private conversation, if you don't mind,' she said firmly, turning quickly back to the telephone before he could reply to her. 'Sorry, John,' she said quietly into the phone.

'Who's with you?'

'It's Francisco, actually. . . .'

'What's he doing there?' John demanded in unusually belligerent tones. 'Did you ask him to stay?'

'No, I did not invite him! In fact I asked him to leave— but he's still here,' she added, shooting a glance to where Francisco lounged in apparent uninterest, his hands in his pockets, gazing out of the window. 'Don't worry about that for now, I can't talk for long. . . . You asked when I was coming home.'

'Have you decided?' John said quietly.

'Mm,' said Liz, with a quick glance towards Francisco. 'I hope . . . I intend to come home tomorrow,' she said firmly, ignoring the muffled exclamation from Francisco's direction.

'I'm so glad!' said John, relief evident in his voice. 'We'll both be looking forward to seeing you. Ring when you get to the local airport and I'll come and collect you.'

'Yes, I'll do that, John. I can't wait to see you both.'

'Or me you! Look after yourself, Liz, until tomorrow,' he added quietly.

'And you. 'Bye,' Liz said, replacing the receiver on the cradle and turning reluctantly to face the silent figure beside her.

'So! That was your lover,' Francisco said, his cold eyes regarding her flushed features contemptuously.

'John is not my lover!' Liz exclaimed, her eyes beginning to sparkle angrily.

'Then perhaps I should call him your fiancé? Although I find it a little difficult to imagine anyone having a fiancé and a husband at one time.'

'I really don't care what you call him, Francisco, providing you understand that I have no intention of withdrawing the divorce suit,' said Liz, raising her chin defiantly. 'And while we're on the subject, as I can't possibly fulfil the requirements of your contract it would be better if I left as soon as possible. I realise it's too late today, but. . . .'

'One moment, Lizbeth!' he said harshly, grasping her arm as she would have moved towards the door. 'If you wish to qualify for the settlement then you must stay here for the whole week, you understand?'

'Yes, I understand very well, Francisco,' she said, shaking his restraining hand angrily from her arm. 'I wouldn't accept a penny of your money if I were starving on the street,' she added, staring proudly at Francisco's arrogant figure.

He raised his eyebrows disbelievingly. 'That may be so! But there is one more thing that I wish to say to you. I have invited a small number of friends for dinner this evening; as you will still also be my guest it would be discourteous if you were not to join us.'

He moved towards the desk and slowly extracted a cigarette from the box, lighting it in a leisurely fashion.

'May I go now?' Liz snapped angrily. 'Have I your permission, my lord?' she said with a mocking curtsey.

'Be careful, Lizbeth!' he grated softly. 'You go too far! You will remember this evening that any rudeness on your part towards me would embarrass our guests.'

'Oh, don't worry, Francisco. I may not be a fit wife for Don Francisco Ramirez de Riera, but I am capable of behaving suitably when the occasion demands it.' With this parting shot Liz walked towards the door and before Francisco had time to reply, she walked out and slammed it violently behind her.

CHAPTER SIX

Liz stayed in her room for the next few hours, overwhelmingly conscious that as a result of her losing her temper with Francisco, final arrangements for her departure tomorrow had not been made. Thoughts of the coming evening depressed her further. Surely Francisco's guests would be embarrassed simply by her presence, the erring wife returned to the fold. Whatever had Francisco told them about her? Liz thought wearily. In all likelihood she would be the most uncomfortable person present. The situation was totally ridiculous!

As the time for dinner approached, she prowled angrily around the room, knowing that if she were to rest it would be one face and one face only that would spring into her mind. Francisco! Angry or contemptuous, but most frequently Francisco as he had looked this afternoon in the pool. . . .

Angrily she thrust the disruptive thoughts aside; maybe if she read for a while that would take her mind off her problems, she thought, reaching into her flight bag for the adventure story bought in the departure lounge for the journey.

She must still have been weary from the journey, because when she awoke the room was full of evening shadows and her watch told her that she had only half an hour to prepare for dinner. Hastily she scrambled off the bed, shedding her clothes on her way to the shower. The cool water on her overheated skin was wonderfully refreshing and she lingered for a few minutes under its invigorating flow.

There was only one possible choice of dress to wear for the evening. Thank goodness she had spent her money extravagantly on the spur of the moment, and bought a beautiful black ankle-length dress especially for this visit. It had been far too expensive, she acknowledged honestly, but it would be a splendid confidence-booster for the coming evening.

After showering she put on her make-up carefully, applying a foundation lightly over skin that was already becomingly tinged with gold; darkening her lashes with carefully applied mascara and shading her eyes skilfully with colour. Her lips were already full and red and barely needed the glowing colour which she applied to them. A light touch of blusher along the cheekbones emphasised their prominence and with her hair fastened in a severe knot she appeared every inch the autocratic Spanish *señora*.

Carefully she stepped into the clinging folds of her evening dress, pulling the shoestring straps into position and smoothing the material over her hips. All resemblance to a severe married lady had fled! The black crêpe clung lovingly to her body, outlining every curve with flattering clarity. The bodice was low, revealing a wide expanse of smooth, gold-tinted skin, and Liz felt a surge of confidence as she realised that she was looking her best.

With one last glance in the full-length mirror she moved slowly towards the door. Now that the time had come to join the other guests her nervousness had visibly increased. She felt as though she was about to enter a room filled with enemies all waiting for her to make a fool of herself. How Francisco would enjoy seeing her humiliated. . . . No! This would not do, she thought with a surge of anguish. Pull yourself together Liz! Show him that you can cope with any situation!

Gradually the wild beating of her heart subsided a little and as she approached the large drawing room she began to take deep, steadying breaths and pushed firmly into the background the wild urge to return to her room and stay there until morning.

From the murmur of voices within the room it was obvious that Francisco's guests had already arrived. Slowly she pushed open the double doors and stood for a moment, poised in the opening. Immediately she became the focus of all eyes and there was a sudden lull in the conversation. Liz felt the ready colour flood into her cheeks, but she raised her chin defiantly, determined not to be overawed by Francisco or his aristocratic friends.

A quick glance around the room showed five unknown faces and then Francisco had moved away from the drinks cabinet and was beside her, immaculate in his evening clothes, an unreadable expression on his dark features. Liz felt an overwhelmingly childish urge to cling to his arm and then he was slowly drawing her forward into the circle of faces.

She found herself responding politely as she was introduced to the two elderly people in the party, but she experienced an immediate surge of antipathy as she came face to face with the cool, uninterested beauty who was their daughter.

Señora Luisa Rodriguez de Macia possessed the pale, flawless complexion that Marisa coveted so longingly; and in her case it was combined with pure, classical features and a heavy mass of luxuriant black hair, secured by diamond-studded combs.

If she was less than pleased to be introduced to Liz her response to Francisco's presence was immediate. He received a glowing, slightly possessive smile and she was rewarded by a charming smile in return, leaving Liz with an almost irresistible urge to slap both their faces.

Francisco appeared reluctant to move away from Señora Rodriguez, but his attention was distracted by the tall man standing beside her.

'Come, Francisco my friend, you may speak to my cousin Luisa at any time. Now it is your duty to introduce me to your so charming and beautiful ... wife.'

Liz sensed the hesitation before the last word and saw

Francisco's mouth tighten a little, although whether in response to this statement or because he had to leave his female guest she could not tell.

'Lizbeth, may I introduce Señor Miguel Diego, a close neighbour.'

'I am very honoured to meet you, *señora*,' Miguel Diego said immediately, staring boldly at her as he bent to bestow a lingering kiss on the back of her hand.

'And I am very pleased to meet you, Señor Diego,' Liz replied in amused tones, instinctively aware that this response would anger Francisco and feeling a fierce urge to make him aware of her.

She deliberately allowed her hand to be retained longer than was necessary, judging by the icy restraint in Francisco's voice as he made the next introduction, that her action had been noted, and no doubt added to the score against her, Liz thought with inward defiance.

'You have not yet met Juan Diego,' Francisco said smoothly, 'the brother of Luisa, and Marisa's affianced husband.'

'How do you do,' said Liz as her hand was once more politely kissed. Her attention momentarily distracted from her own problems, she looked carefully at Marisa's future husband. The relationship with Luisa was perfectly obvious. He was certainly a handsome young man, she conceded, and there was a distinct twinkle in his eye as he returned her scrutiny.

'Marisa tells me that you and she are now good friends,' he said. 'Do I pass the test as Marisa's future husband?' he added in amused tones, bowing elaborately from the waist.

'If I had to have my husband chosen for me by my family, I would be quite pleased that they had chosen you,' Liz told him with disconcerting candour, the hot colour rushing into her cheeks as she realised the full enormity of her words.

There were sharp gasps of shock from the direction of

Juan's family and then both Juan and Miguel began to laugh. Liz was overwhelmingly conscious of Francisco's icy disapproval as she began to stammer out rather disjointed apologies.

'I'm ... I'm ... terribly sorry, Señor Diego! I just wasn't thinking. That was terribly rude of me!'

'Please, say no more,' Juan Diego replied with a smile. 'You disapprove of our methods of choosing partners, but you approve the choice made for Marisa. I am flattered! Have no fear, had I not loved Marisa I would never have consented to marry her,' he added with an amused glance at his parents' shocked faces. 'You need have no fears, we shall be very happy,' he added, walking towards the younger girl and drawing her arm gently through his own.

Liz felt an overwhelming sense of loss as she saw the loving look he bestowed on Marisa. Had Francisco ever looked at her that way? She couldn't remember. . . . Involuntarily she glanced up at his face, to find her eyes held by the brooding anger in his own. She felt her legs begin to tremble at the malevolence in his gaze and she knew that she would have given way to her distress and further condemned herself in his eyes had not help come from an unexpected quarter.

'Come along, *querido*, let us go in to dinner,' Luisa Rodriguez murmured, clinging persuasively to Francisco's arm, endeavouring to draw his attention back to herself. For a moment Liz thought he would shake the other woman away and chastise his wife publicly, in front of his guests; but his self-control seemed to reassert itself and with a visible struggle he responded to the Spanish woman's invitation.

'*Si! Si*, dinner will be ready,' he said, the suppressed anger still evident in his tone. 'Please, come.'

Liz's attention was claimed by both Miguel Diego and Carlos as they asked to take her in to dinner. Now that she was no longer in Francisco's overwhelming pres-

ence some of her natural resilience reasserted itself. Had
Francisco had any feeling for her at all she realised that
he would have attempted to minimise her offence. This
knowledge caused a spark of revolt to grow stronger within
her. He only cared about his damned reputation! Appearances were everything to him, Liz thought angrily, a
determination to make him suffer growing with every
moment.

'Why don't you both take me in to dinner?' she said
recklessly, smiling warmly at the two men. If she had
shocked the other guests earlier she was really going to
give them something to talk about now, she decided, the
grim determination within her belied by the warmth with
which she received the attentions of Carlos and
Miguel.

Again there was an uncomfortable silence as she entered
the room on the arms of her escorts; but she forced herself
to ignore everything but the two men vying for her attention. The lights around the room were low, the table lit
by elegant stands of candles, casting flickering shadows
across its occupants.

Liz glanced momentarily away from her two com-
panions, only to encounter the brooding malevolence of
Francisco's gaze. Inwardly she was horrified at her own
behaviour, knowing that she was playing Carlos against
Miguel in an unforgivable manner. Her laughter was
too loud and too frequent and she sensed that conversation
between the other dinner guests was forced and uncertain.

Luisa Rodriguez sat near to Francisco, a look of aristocratic disdain on her proud features, and Liz felt an even
greater urge to shock her. Recklessly she raised her glass
to Miguel and drained its contents, making no demur
as he lifted her hand once more to his lips and bestowed a
lingering kiss on her overheated skin.

She was aware of Carlos glowering beside her, but her
conscience had begun to prick her with regard to the

younger man. Instinctively she sensed that to Miguel this was merely a game; his response to any attractive woman, combined with a spirit of pure mischief. Not so with Carlos, and she knew that she must not encourage him further.

'Coffee will be served in the drawing room,' said Francisco, his harsh voice interrupting Liz's thoughts.

'Come, Liz, you must sit next to me,' Miguel said, smiling at Carlos's angry expression; only to find his quarry removed from his grasp by an icily controlled Francisco.

'See to our guests, Carlos!' Francisco snapped, his cruel grasp on Liz's arm effectively preventing her escape. 'You will excuse my wife for the moment, Diego. We have things to discuss. . . . We will rejoin you later.'

As the two men retired into the drawing room, closing the door behind them Liz wrenched her arm from Francisco's grasp, examining the already livid bruising with angry eyes.

'You really are a beast, aren't you, Francisco? You just can't resist throwing your weight around. . . .'

'Let us leave my personality out of this discussion for the moment,' Francisco said in harsh tones. 'It is your behaviour which we should be questioning. What the hell do you think you are playing at? You wish to ruin my reputation in front of my friends?' he added, staring at her with angry eyes.

Liz flinched as he gave vent to a low-voiced tirade of insults and she tried to step backwards as he reached for her upper arms with hands that trembled slightly. But she was not quick enough to escape and only succeeded in stumbling slightly so that her whole weight was thrown against Francisco's body.

She had a startlingly clear view of his immaculate linen and of the small muscle which throbbed uncontrollably beside his upper lip, then she was firmly propelled away from him and forced to grip the dining chair for support.

'Ah no! Those tactics will not avail you on this occasion, Lizbeth! You are still a beautiful woman and I concede that as a beautiful woman you can still make me desire you. But. . . .'

'Why, you . . . you arrogant, self-opinionated swine of a man! If you think I would ever do anything to deliberately attract your . . . your . . . attentions, you're very much mistaken!' Liz paused for breath a moment, clenching her fists at her side in an effort to stop their trembling. The enormity of his suggestion filled her with horror, and yet the most distressing thing was that she was not sure that his accusation was completely without foundation.

'Oh no!' she said on a trembling breath as Francisco would have spoken. 'Oh no! I've listened to quite enough from you, Francisco Ramirez. You always were a self-centred, opinionated devil, and time has obviously not mellowed you. The only thing you care about is the reputation of yourself and your family. The opinion of others is all-important to you,' she finished, her whole body trembling with emotion. 'If you had any compassion or pity in your heart you would have tried to help me back there,' she said, nodding towards the drawing room where the other guests waited. 'It was not my intention to embarrass Marisa or her fiancé. I was nervous—uncertain; the room was not exactly filled with people who had my best interests at heart. . . . Oh, what's the use!' she groaned in anguished tones as he continued to stare at her, his face implacable in the dim light. 'What do you care? The sooner I can put you out of my life for good, the better,' she sighed, turning away from him and walking quickly towards the closed doors. Each moment she expected to be dragged forcibly back into the room and made to pay for her defiance; but there was complete silence from the figure behind her.

As she entered the drawing room there was a studious lowering of heads. Only Marisa came towards her, a sympathetic expression on her face, and drew her towards the couch where she and Juan were sitting.

'Come and sit down, Lizbeth. You are a little upset, I think?'

'No, no,' Liz demurred quietly. 'Just angry. Francisco and I always have that effect on one another,' she added with an apologetic glance in Juan's direction. 'Look, I really am sorry about the things I said earlier; they . . . they just slipped out— but that's no excuse, I know. You were very good about it,' she added quietly.

Juan shrugged. 'Why should I be otherwise? I was not offended. A little shocked at first, yes . . . but it was not such a terrible thing to say, and I am forced to agree that our methods of choosing our children's partners can be a little . . . unreasonable. I was fortunate,' he said with a smile, taking Marisa's hand into his own. 'The partner chosen for me was the one I would have chosen myself.'

'I too am fortunate,' Marisa said quietly. 'I am very glad that you spoke as you did tonight, Lizbeth. I had not realised until this evening how deeply I cared for Juan, nor did I know that he loved me. . . . For us you have made it very much better.'

'Well, it's nice to be receiving thanks from one member of the Ramirez family, at any rate,' Liz added with a forced laugh. 'And if you're wondering where Francisco is, I haven't a clue, but he's not laid out on the dining room carpet with your priceless china in pieces around him—although I must confess that I was tempted.

'I did not think it,' said Marisa. 'But your parents must think his absence very odd, Juan? Carlos is looking quite harassed.'

'Where is Miguel?' Liz interposed a shade defiantly.

'He is in the garden,' said Marisa, and after a moment: 'He is a handsome man I know, Lizbeth, but you must not take him too seriously. He has a reputation among those who know him as a heartbreaker, a . . .a philanderer. Is that the word?'

'Oh, don't worry! I'm immune!' Liz replied with a laugh, inwardly marvelling that Marisa should find Miguel handsome when she had her brothers as models. His face was already beginning to slacken at the jowls and he would be distinctly corpulent before too long, Liz thought, unable to resist comparing his softness unfavourably with the harsh, unforgiving planes of Francisco's face.

'I shall go in search of Francisco,' Luisa Rodriguez said, breaking into Liz's musings. 'He will be in his study, I think.'

'What is Luisa Rodriguez to Francisco?' Liz asked abruptly, as the other woman left the room.

'It was thought at one time that she would marry him,' Marisa said a little hesitantly.

'Yes, I know. Before I came along. Were they formally engaged?'

'No. Francisco always insisted that he would make his own choice, he would never be hurried into anything.'

'That figures!' Liz said drily.

Marisa shrugged. 'It was always understood that they would marry one day.'

'But what now?' Liz persisted. 'She is married, is that so?'

'My sister is a widow,' Juan said quietly.

'I'm sorry—I always seem to be saying the wrong thing. I'd forgotten that she's your sister.'

Juan raised his broad shoulders dismissively. 'We do not always see eye to eye, but—well, as to what she and Francisco intend in the future I cannot say. It may be that if you divorce him they would marry, but my sister is a devout Catholic. . . .'

'If Francisco asks her she will marry him,' Marisa said firmly. She shot Liz a glance and added: 'I cannot tell whether Francisco intends to ask her.'

'They seem to be getting along well enough at the present moment,' Liz said tonelessly, her stomach contracting painfully as she watched Luisa and Francisco enter the room, Luisa clinging persuasively to Francisco's arm, her slim body close to his side and he smiling down at her with complete attention, no trace now on his face of his earlier anger.

Determinedly Liz forced herself to look away from their imposing figures. Why, oh, why, when Francisco treated her so badly, did he have this disrupting effect on her senses? Even in the middle of their fiercest arguments she knew that she was not immune from his personality. Physical attraction has a lot to answer for, she thought wearily, only to jump slightly as Miguel materialised behind her and laid a possessive hand on her arm.

'You have returned! I am glad, the room was empty without your presence.'

'Oh, really?' said Liz in laughing disbelief. 'How would you know, when you were in the garden?'

'Ah, but I could not bear this room without you,' Miguel protested dramatically.

'I see,' Liz laughed. 'Well, I forgive you—are you going to sit down?'

'But no. If you will permit we will take a walk in the garden. It is beautiful this evening ... and warm,' he added as she hesitated uncertainly. She shot a glance at Francisco and immediately determined to accept Miguel's invitation. He and Luisa were sitting close together in intimate conversation, Francisco's head almost touching the woman's glossy hair as he bent to listen to her.

'Yes, if you wish, I'll come,' she said in strained tones.

Miguel apparently did not notice Liz's distinct lack of enthusiasm and he led her possessively towards the opened french windows, into the lush, closely planted gardens, guiding her down one of the narrow gravel paths leading away from the house.

'Wait! Wait a moment!' Liz protested, pulling her arm from his grasp. 'This is a walk in the garden, not an elopement!'

'But naturally,' Miguel replied with a self-possessed smile. 'Along this path there is a small garden, heavy with the perfumes of the evening. . . .'

'Fine, but let's go more slowly, if you don't mind.' She pointed to her high, strappy sandals. 'These were not made for running along gravel paths.'

'A thousand apologies!' Miguel dropped down on to his haunches on the rough gravel, taking one of her resisting feet in both his hands. 'You are in pain, shall I carry you?'

'No, thank you!' Liz said hastily, beginning to regret her decision to take a walk with Miguel. 'Look, I think it would probably be more sensible if we went back to the house . . .'

'Please—I shall be heartbroken if you return to the house! We can walk along the terrace if you do not trust yourself alone with me.'

'Okay, you win, we'll go and look at this garden . . . but more slowly, please, I don't want to break an ankle.'

Fortunately the path widened a little as it wound among the exotic vegetation; but Liz began to be more than a little uncertain as to Miguel's intentions as they showed no sign of reaching their destination.

'Where is this garden, Miguel? I think we ought to be getting back, we must be miles from the house by now,' she said, realising suddenly just how foolish her actions had been. After her behaviour at dinner this evening, Miguel would no doubt think her ripe for his lovemaking, and even if she shouted for assistance it was doubtful if anyone at the house would hear. In any event that in itself would cause further scandal and confirm everyone's worst suspicions of her dubious character, Liz thought wearily.

'Only another few steps,' Miguel urged, 'and then you will see.'

'Lead on—I just want to rest my feet; you did say there was a seat?' Liz added, then gave a gasp of pure pleasure as they rounded the final bend.

They had entered a small garden, surrounded by thick, dark green hedges. The white-painted arbour in the background was fronted by a softly splashing fountain and its walls were clad in a riot of bougainvillea and heavily scented roses.

'Come, there is a seat in the arbour where you can rest.'

Liz sank with relief on to the wrought iron seat, wishing she could throw caution to the winds and bathe her feet in the refreshing water of the fountain. She really ought to have worn more sensible shoes, she thought, raising her feet to inspect the offending articles, but she was forced to admit that this pair looked extremely elegant.

She began to regret that the seat was big enough for two as she felt Miguel place himself beside her, sliding his arm casually along the back of the seat. She immediately leaned forward, pretending to admire the perfect shape of the passion flower, twining itself around the elegant pillars of the arbour.

'Relax, *querida*! You need have no fears that we shall be overlooked here. As you so rightly said, we are many minutes' walk away from the house. In any case,' he added, with an indolent shrug, 'your husband is well occupied with my cousin, why should he come looking for you? She tells me that you are to be divorced in any event.'

'It is true that I intend to divorce Francisco,' Liz agreed, turning to face Miguel and trying to remain calm in the face of his ardent expression. After all, she told herself, he had every reason to expect more than conversation after her disgraceful behaviour at dinner this evening. Aloud she continued: 'I have, however, already promised to marry someone else; and whatever you may think, whatever impression I may have given, I'm not in the habit of playing fast and loose—of being unfaithful,' she amended, as she saw his puzzled expression.

'You tell me this,' Miguel complained in frankly dis-believing tones, 'and yet I understand that you have a son ... and not Francisco's son, I think, otherwise he would be in residence at Riera at this moment.'

'Francisco told you that?'

'Does it matter how I know? It is true, is it not?'

'I think you should mind your own business,' said Liz, rising quickly to her feet and walking towards the path, all her sympathy towards Miguel vanishing with this last disclosure.

'One moment, *señora!*' Miguel said, gripping her arm to prevent her escape, an angry expression on his softly, handsome features. 'You led me to believe that you would be more than willing to respond to my advances, and respond you will,' he said, forcibly turning her unyielding body to face his own. 'I do not like to be taken for a ride!'

'Let me go, you ... you brute!' Liz gasped, struggling ineffectually to loosen his grip on her arms. 'When I tell Francisco what you've done he'll make you pay....'

'After your behaviour this evening?' he said with a mocking laugh. 'Do you think he will believe that you were unwilling? Oh no, *querida!* I can do what I will with you and no one will protest.' So saying he dragged her wrists firmly behind her back and pulled her still strug-gling body close to his own.

Momentarily Liz marvelled at the differing sensations that such an action could accomplish. When Francisco held her so, her whole body melted with living fire; and yet all she felt at the moment was complete revulsion, combined with fear, she acknowledged honestly. Oh, if only Francisco would come! she begged silently, turning her face roughly away as Miguel attempted to force his lips on to hers.

'Francisco! Francisco! Help!' she shouted desperately, continuing to struggle against her captor, aware that she was not achieving anything except to anger Miguel further. 'Let me go! Oh, let me go!' she gasped, turning her head this way and that to escape his demanding mouth.

'There is no escape! Why not relax and enjoy it?' Miguel retorted with a cruel laugh. 'I have never had any complaints in the past.' Gripping her arms with only one of his own, he attempted to turn her face towards his with the other; 'Keep still, woman,' he muttered, taking a painful grasp on her hair and causing her to wince with pain.

'Let me go! You mustn't do this!' Liz sobbed distractedly, tears beginning to course down her cheeks as he forced his mouth over her own unyielding lips.

'Let my wife go, Diego!'

Released abruptly from Miguel's cruel grip, Liz felt herself falling weakly to the ground. It was Francisco's hard grip that supported her and helped her to regain her balance.

'Francisco, listen to me—please!'

'Go back to the house, Lizbeth!' Francisco ordered harshly, disregarding her interruption. 'You can go through the inner courtyard and straight to my study. Make sure you are not seen . . . you are not a pretty sight,' he added with cruel candour. 'Go now! I have business to attend to here,' he said, staring grimly at Miguel Diego's half mocking, half wary figure.

'What are you going to do? Oh no, just let him go!' Liz begged, gripping Francisco's arm urgently. 'No harm was done, Francisco. Don't make things worse, please!'

'Just go, Lizbeth!' Francisco said harshly. Removing her fingers forcibly from his arm and turning to regard her with a face devoid of emotion. 'If you are wise you will wait for me in my study. If I have to search for you again it will make me . . . very angry.'

With one last glance at the two silent figures behind her Liz stumbled along the path to the house, praying desperately that Francisco would not be hurt. She knew from bitter experience that Miguel's indolent pose was deceptive and that his body possessed surprising strength.

When she reached Francisco's study she sank wearily on to one of the comfortable armchairs, prey to a bewildering number of emotions. She did not even know whether the other guests were still in the house, or if Francisco had asked them to leave before going in search of her.

Why, oh, why had she ever come to Spain? Even if she returned home tomorrow there was no going back to the comfortable existence that she had had before this visit. The shock of this latest episode had made her painfully aware of the futility of trying to live with any man but Francisco.

The disturbing thoughts whirled unceasingly around her brain, giving her no respite. She was forced to admit that she was still as much in love with Francisco as she had ever been and life without him stretched out before her as an endless barren wilderness. Perhaps it would be better to beg Francisco to take her back even without love, than to have to face the future completely without him. He had admitted that he still found her desirable, maybe if she told him the truth about Edward he would accept her into his life again.

Wearily she rested her forehead on her folded arms, marking the highly polished surface of his desk with the tears which trickled unheeded down her cheeks. Even in this weakened state she realised that she was still too proud to beg. She would just have to make the best of her life as it was. At least she still had Edward to love, she acknowledged thankfully.

'So! You were wise to stay, Lizbeth wise not to anger me further this evening!'

'Oh, you startled me!' Liz gasped, endeavouring to wipe the tears from her cheeks with the back of her hand.

'Use this,' Francisco said drily. 'You may feel the need for it again after I have said what I intend. . . .'

'Oh no, Francisco! Please!' Liz protested weakly. 'I

know I've been all kinds of a fool this evening. I've disgraced myself in front of your guests and the woman you love. I know I've been a bitch, but you'll be rid of me tomorrow and you need never see me again. Can't we just leave it at that?' she finished, leaning her head back against the seat and closing her eyes in an attempt to shut out the contempt and anger in his own.

'No, we cannot leave it at that, as you so conveniently wish,' Francisco ground out harshly. 'If you think to persuade me to agree to a divorce by your sluttish behaviour, then I must tell you that you have failed. I have long been aware that your standard of morals is not high. . . .'

'How dare you!' Liz gasped, shocked out of her lethargy by his cruel words.

'I dare because it is true,' said Francisco, reaching into the pocket of his close-fitting jacket and withdrawing his cigarette case. He lit a cigarette impatiently, savouring the first lungfuls of smoke with obvious enjoyment.

'I would have thought that even you would have had more sense of what is fitting than to tell Diego about your illegitimate son. Assuming, of course, that your cries for help were genuine,' he added, raising his brows interrogatively.

'You heard, then? I wondered . . . I hoped. . . .' Liz stammered softly. 'But I didn't tell Miguel about Ed . . . my son, he already knew. I assumed that you had. . . .'

'You think that I would ever speak of such a thing?' Francisco said bitterly, and after a pause added: 'However, I can imagine how the knowledge has spread. My family know about your son, of course, and Madre is a good friend of Señora Diego,' he shrugged wearily. 'They have no doubt spent many happy hours discussing how much better my life would have been had I married Luisa as they wished.' He turned away from Liz as though he found the sight distasteful, and stared in brooding silence out into the shadowy courtyard.

'I doubt whether Diego will ever mention the subject

again, certainly not in my presence,' he said grimly.

'Did you . . . did you hurt him?' asked Liz, rising from her seat at the desk and walking towards his still figure, noticing for the first time the beginnings of a livid bruise that marked his left cheekbone.

'He'll survive,' Francisco said coldly, raising his hand unconsciously and exploring his jawline, wincing momentarily as his fingers came away covered with blood.

'You *are* hurt! Let me look!' Liz turned his face gently, to examine the ragged cut above his jaw.

'Diego favours rings,' Francisco observed with distaste. 'Leave it! It doesn't matter,' he said impatiently, as Liz attempted to dab the wound rather ineffectually with his own handkerchief. 'Later!' he said again, placing his hands on her upper arms and propelling her firmly away from him. 'He has spoiled your dress,' he added dispassionately, raising his hand to touch the ragged tear disfiguring the soft material. 'A pity! You looked . . . attractive in it.'

'Th-thank you,' Liz murmured, increasingly conscious of the effect that his proximity was having on her metabolism, the rapid beating of her heart and the betraying warmth spreading with alarming swiftness through her body. His touch on her arms was at once a pain and a pleasure, and she felt her already weakened self-control moving towards breaking point.

'We have still to discuss your behaviour this evening,' Francisco said abruptly.

'I don't know what else I can say. I behaved badly and I'm truly sorry. You have every right to be angry, Francisco . . . I know.'

'You think that is all?' Francisco muttered in distinctly husky tones. 'You do not think that perhaps you should be made to pay for making me suffer?' he added, his grip on her upper arms tightening cruelly.

'Please, Francisco,' Liz whispered, raising her hands to

his chest, unable to disguise the weakening emotion turning her limbs to water.

With an almost animal growl he dragged her unresisting body against his own, and she no longer even pretended to repel his advances. Her arms twined sinuously around his neck so that her fingers were buried in his hair, and she arched her body close to his, holding nothing back in her newly acknowledged love for him.

'*Dios*, Lizbeth, I want you!' he groaned, trailing his lips sensuously over the soft skin of her shoulders, smoothing away her offending shoulder straps with an unsteady hand and devouring her mouth with his own, like a starving man suddenly presented with a banquet.

'Oh, Francisco, Francisco! Please, love me!'

'Your dress—help me,' Francisco muttered huskily, struggling for a moment with the zip, finally propelling it downwards, allowing the silken folds to fall in a heap around her ankles.

Momentarily Liz felt a twinge of fear at her actions. She realised that this was a purely physical attraction on Francisco's part and that there was no future in it for her. Well, at least she would have this to remember, she thought defiantly, no longer willing to listen to the dictates of her own good sense, and with hands that trembled slightly she loosened the buttons of his shirt, sliding her arms around his lean muscled body, her breasts pressing softly against his naked chest.

'*Cristo*, you are beautiful! I had not remembered just how beautiful. Let me look at you, Lizbeth,' Francisco murmured huskily, pushing her gently away from his body and bending to place his lips on her hardened nipples; his thick black hair brushing her soft skin and sending shivers of desire through her body.

'Francisco, Francisco! Are you there?' The peremptory knocking on the study door shattered Liz's rose-coloured dream, and with a shocked gasp she pulled herself out of Francisco's arms.

'The door . . . it's Marisa!'

'Let her wait,' Francisco muttered, his voice husky with emotion. With a groan he pulled her tense figure into his arms once again. 'The door is locked. . . .' His voice trailed away as he began to caress her neck with his tongue, moving expert hands over her once familiar body; weakening her flimsy resistance so that she was soon soft and clinging to him once more.

'You must answer,' she whispered a little desperately, as the knocking persisted and Francisco continued to plunder her mouth with his own.

'I know you are in the study, Francisco . . . you must come! Your guests are leaving . . . please come!' Marisa called in low, urgent tones, sounding very close to tears as she added: 'Juan's parents are very angry. Please, Francisco!'

With a low groan Francisco detached himself from Liz's arms. 'One moment, Marisa, ask them to wait a moment. . . . I will be with you. Go!' he reiterated loudly as there was no movement from the hallway. 'I will follow.'

There were sounds of hurrying feet on the hall tiles as Marisa returned to the drawing room and Francisco began to fumble with the buttons of his shirt with hands that trembled alarmingly. 'No, I can manage,' he said in strained tones, holding up his hand in a dismissive gesture as Liz would have moved to help him.

For a moment she stood without moving, hurt by his apparent rejection of her, unknowingly provocative, her hair in wild disorder around her shoulders, her skin still soft and glowing from his lovemaking.

'*Dios*, I cannot manage,' he muttered. 'You will have to help me. But put on your dress first, if you please, otherwise I do not think that I shall be able to leave this room.' The eyes which he raised to her own were still dark with passion and Liz felt the familiar weakness run through her body. 'Please, Lizbeth, don't look at me that way!'

'I ... I'm coming,' she murmured softly, pulling the dishevelled dress quickly over her slim body, the hot colour flooding her cheeks as she felt the intensity of his gaze. Carefully avoiding his eyes, she fastened the offending buttons, smoothing his lapels and brushing his shoulders carefully.

'Your face—it's still bleeding. You don't look very respectable. . . .'

'There is blood on your face also; and on your shoulders and your breast,' he murmured softly, trailing his fingers gently from one area to the next, causing her to tremble uncontrollably beneath his touch.

'I must go!' he said then, straightening abruptly, his heavy-lidded eyes successfully hiding any indication of his feelings. 'My guests must accept my face as it is. It will at least provide an explanation for my continued absence.'

After Francisco had left the room Liz stood for a moment in silent abstraction, savouring the memory of those last few minutes, bitterly regretting Marisa's interruption. She was in no doubt about the outcome of their lovemaking had Marisa not intervened. But she was forced to concede that perhaps it was better so.

It was true that Francisco appeared to desire her body as much as he had ever done, but his opinion of her personality, formed so arbitrarily all those years ago, had not altered one iota. All his gentler feelings were spent on his family ... and also on Luisa Rodriguez, Liz acknowledged painfully.

She must go before he decided to return to the room, she decided swiftly. There was no future for her here and the sooner she accepted the fact, the better. Francisco seemed to think that she went haphazardly from one sexual encounter to another, and nothing would ever make him believe that he was the only lover she had ever had ... or wanted.

His suspicions had never been true, but he had never

given her the benefit of the doubt. He had always put the worst possible connotation on her actions. Perhaps the gap in their upbringing and life-styles had just been too wide to bridge; the only true point of contact between them had been their mutual physical attraction.

Automatically Liz began to tidy herself, wetting Francisco's handkerchief, which she still held in her hand, rubbing fiercely at the offending bloodstains, and smoothing her dress with hands that were still unsteady. Reluctantly she decided that nothing could be done about her hair, and she removed the few remaining pins and allowed it to fall in silken swathes around her shoulders.

Fortunately the corridor was deserted as she left Francisco's study, but she felt a distinct trembling in her lower limbs when she heard voices issuing from the drawing room. She had no wish to meet the accusing stare of her fellow guests or experience the aristocratic disdain of Luisa Rodriguez this evening. She placed her feet carefully on the lower steps of the staircase, quelling a rather hysterical desire to laugh as she wondered what the servants would think if they could see her at this moment.

There was still no movement from the drawing room and with a gasp of relief she reached the upper landing, hurrying into her room and bolting the door in silent defiance. Although what she would do if Francisco asked for admittance she didn't like to consider.

She thrust those thoughts firmly aside. A bath was obviously the next essential, and when she eventually relaxed in the soothing depths, the disasters and delights of the day began to drift away. . . .

Abruptly she sat up and jumped out in one movement, aware that she had almost fallen asleep in the caressing warmth of the water. Suicide by drowning was definitely not on the agenda, she decided, particularly not in that over-perfumed water. She wrinkled her nose distastefully and began to rub her body briskly with the towel until it glowed.

Then she stood for a moment in front of the full-length mirror, gazing at the slim vulnerable figure reflected within. Her body was as it had always been, there was nothing in the reflection to remind her of Francisco's demanding lovemaking—only the faint bruises on her upper arms, and they could have been made by Miguel, she acknowledged with a barely suppressed shudder.

Hastily pulling a bathrobe around her slender body, she turned off the bathroom light and walked across the cool tiled floor towards the welcoming bed. As she closed her eyes wearily her thoughts drifted naturally to Edward, but another, more shadowy face persisted in intruding. Slowly they blended together, those faces, so alike, so dear to her, joining and fading, one gay, one sad. . . .

CHAPTER SEVEN

Liz awoke with a start to find her body dripping with sweat and the bedroom light still burning fiercely. Wearily she reached for the pull switch and turned off the tormenting light, her whole body aching with unfulfilled longings. She sighed and turned over restlessly, thinking it unlikely that she would get off to sleep again.

When she next awoke the sun was shining brightly through the windows and there was an appetising smell of coffee from the small tray on the bedside table. Ana must have just left, Liz thought, struggling quickly into an upright position and reaching for her watch from the bedside table.

'Dear God! It's eleven o'clock!'

Without further hesitation she hurried out of bed, hastily drinking a cup of the invigorating liquid provided, the question of whether she would still have time to reach England running round and round in her brain. She washed hurriedly, slipping into a sleeveless red blouse and a simple navy skirt, throwing the jacket which completed the outfit casually on to the bed.

She would ask Ana to send one of the girls to pack for her while she ate a hasty breakfast and finalised her departure arrangements, she decided, relaxing a little now that her immediate plan of action was clear in her mind. With accomplished expertise she pinned her hair into a knot, and slipping a pair of high-heeled but comfortable shoes on to her feet, made her way towards the dining room.

There were no other members of the family in the vicinity when she reached the lower floor and the dining room too was deserted. Liz was forced to admit to herself that she was relieved at not having to face anyone, although how she was to accomplish her departure without them was not clear. She shrugged fatalistically. She would manage somehow, she determined inwardly, turning to smile pleasantly at the young maid who came to ask for her breakfast order.

'Oh, some fruit juice, rolls and coffee, I think, please, Pilar. Oh, and would you ask Ana if I might speak to her when I've finished?'

'*Si, señora*, I will do so.'

Liz stretched and sighed after the girl had left the room. It was going to be very difficult making all the necessary arrangements through Ana. It was obvious that Francisco had not the slightest intention of complying with her request to leave today. After the events of last night he would probably think she had changed her mind anyway, Liz acknowledged honestly.

Ana's fresh rolls and preserves were delicious and Liz ate them ravenously. She had been too keyed up at dinner the previous evening to eat very much and she had not realised just how hungry she had become.

'You are enjoying your meal *señora*? You have eaten all the rolls, that is good! Soon you will have more flesh on your bones,' the housekeeper said in satisfied tones.

'That was delicious!' Liz answered honestly. 'Did Pilar tell you that I had something I wanted to ask?' She was uncertain how best to approach Ana with her request for transport to Seville, now that the moment had arrived.'

'*Si, señora*, but first I must tell you that you have a visitor.'

'A visitor?'

'*Si*. Señora Rodriguez is waiting in the drawing room. I have taken her some coffee. . . .'

'Are you sure that it's me she wants to see, and not Francisco?' Liz interposed in puzzled tones.

'*Si*, I am sure, *señora*! I tell her that the Señor inspects the vines today, but she knows this already,' Ana stated with a characteristic shrug. 'It was you that she asked to see.'

'Er . . . where are Marisa and Carlos?'

'Señorita Marisa is visiting Señora Diego today, and the young Señor is with Don Francisco.'

'I see. Well, thank you, Ana. I will go to the drawing room directly.'

'You wished to speak to me about something else, *señora*? You have a complaint to make? One of the girls has made a mistake?'

'No—oh no, nothing like that! Perhaps I could speak to you when Señora Rodriguez has left?'

'*Si! Si, senora.*'

As the ample figure of the housekeeper retreated from the room Liz wrinkled her forehead in frowning concentration, in a futile attempt to think of one single reason to explain Luisa Rodriguez's visit. Shaking her head in irritation, she left the sanctuary of the breakfast room and hurried along the tiled hall towards the more formal surroundings of the drawing room. Liz was forced to admit that Luisa Rodriguez was the last person she had hoped to see on her final morning at Riera—the woman to whom Francisco would soon be married.

Angrily she pushed the unwelcome thoughts aside, taking a deep breath before pushing open the double doors to the drawing room. The Spanish woman looked just as beautiful and elegant in the harsh light of morning as she had the evening before. She was formally dressed in a beige-coloured dress and jacket, the obligatory string of perfectly matched pearls around her slender throat.

'Forgive me for not greeting you earlier,' Liz said more calmly than she felt, knowing instinctively that this visit would be an unpleasant one for her.

'It is no matter. Ana told me that you had only just risen,' Luisa said fastidiously, her cold eyes flicking over Liz like a snake preparing to strike.

Liz suppressed an inward shudder, certain now that

Luisa intended her only ill. 'I don't wish to be rude, Señora Rodriguez, but shall we get to the point of your visit? I can't honestly believe that you have come here to make a social call—not to me, at any rate; and as Ana told you, Francisco is not at home at the moment.'

'This I already knew,' Luisa answered with a dismissive gesture. 'Francisco told me yesterday that he would be in the vineyard today. And as you so rightly say, I would not normally pay a social call on someone . . . like you!'

Liz gave a small gasp at the sheer effrontery of the woman.

'I assure you that I could have survived very well without this visit, but as you are here, shall we get on? I have things to do.'

Luisa Rodriguez shot a malevolent glance in Liz's direction but forbore to comment, resuming her seat with studied grace and picking up her coffee cup slowly.

'Shall we sit down? This may take some time.'

'Like I said, I have things to do,' Liz answered quietly, looking at her watch with obvious impatience.

'Nevertheless I feel sure that you will wish to hear what I have to tell you. Something which I feel sure you ought to hear—for your own good, you understand?'

'I am pleased to hear that you have my best interests at heart, *señora*.'

The other woman coloured angrily under Liz's mocking stare, and putting down her coffee cup she gathered together her bag and gloves and stood facing Liz's wary figure.

'In the normal course of events I do not pretend that I would make any attempt to help you. . . . But I believe this unsuitable marriage between you and Francisco has more than run its course. And, while I understand why he would wish to prolong it a little in order to gain his revenge. . . .'

She paused a moment to regard Liz with undisguised hatred, obviously savouring the other girl's discomfiture.

'Let's not play games, shall we?' Liz interposed in calm tones, amazed that her voice could sound so unconcerned, when inwardly her stomach was churning alarmingly. 'Why should prolonging our marriage help Francisco to gain his revenge? I would have thought that nine years of being tied to a woman you hated would be long enough for anyone!' She walked away from Luisa and turned to stare unseeingly out of the window. 'Now, if you've finished what you came to tell me. . . .'

'Oh, but I have not finished! I understand that Francisco is paying you to remain here and that you must stay a full week to obtain the money? Is that not so?' After a moment's pause Luisa added, 'You choose to remain silent on this matter. Perhaps even you are capable of some sense of shame! But I am sure of my facts in this. You see, Francisco himself told me of the arrangement.' As Liz would have interrupted she held up her hand in a dismissive gesture. 'Let me finish, *señora*, if you please! It would be far better for all concerned if you left the *estancia*—today, before the others return. You need not fear that you will lose money by so doing,' she hurried on. 'I will see that you receive adequate recompense. I am well able to match any sum that Francisco offered, believe me!' Quickly she retrieved a small gold pen and cheque book from her bag. 'Name your price!' she said in contemptuous tones.

Liz began to feel a growing sense of anger. Did all these people really believe that money could buy anything?

'Why should I take money from you, *señora*? If I stay here another few days I can, as you so rightly surmise, collect a substantial sum from Francisco. And these are hardly unpleasant surroundings in which to pass the time, you must agree?'

'You are reluctant to leave? Perhaps Francisco is already succeeding in his plan,' Luisa added with a cruel laugh. 'Oh, come now, *señora*! You really are naïve, are you not? You did not really think that Francisco could have any personal interest in you after all these years? Oh, I grant that some men would find you attractive,' she raked Liz with a scathing glance and added: 'It has been Francisco's intention to make you fall in love with him again—you have been easy game, believe me!' As Liz would have protested she added with cruel candour: 'How do you think that I know all these details, eh? Francisco has told me, of course!

'After you are divorced we shall marry and I shall be to him everything that a wife should be ... everything that you are not. I shall leave you now,' she finished, glancing with barely concealed triumph at Liz's pale features framed in the light from the window. 'I feel very sorry for you, *señora*. To have gained such a rich and powerful husband as Don Francisco and then to lose him! It is very sad for you.'

Liz made no attempt to escort her unwelcome visitor to the door, but remained standing in the window embrasure as Señora Rodriguez opened the drawing room doors and clicked over the hall tiles towards the courtyard. When the footsteps had finally receded and a car engine sprang powerfully into life, she gave a long shuddering sigh and buried her face in hands that trembled with emotion.

Francisco's actions had not even been caused by desire, simply an urge to revenge himself upon her. She groaned softly. What a fool she had been, what a fund of amusement she must have caused him! How he and Luisa would laugh when he disclosed what an easy conquest she had been last evening!

On this thought she calmed herself a little. Whatever Luisa Rodriguez had to say on the subject she felt sure that Francisco would never reveal the more intimate details of their lovemaking to his intended bride. She got the distinct impression that Luisa would not be amused by every aspect of the situation.

At least Luisa's disclosure made her decision to leave Spain a great deal easier ... or did it? Did she really want to give Señora Rodriguez the satisfaction of seeing her turn tail and run away? Liz stiffened her shoulders imperceptibly at the thought. That would surely be playing directly into the Spanish woman's hands. If only she could carry it through it would be better to stay for the week as planned and appear unimpressed by Francisco's advances, and at least not give him the satisfaction of knowing that he had hurt her.

'The Señora has gone?' Liz jumped slightly as Ana's familiar tone's disturbed her reverie. 'You are not well, *señora*! It is the heat, perhaps. Come, please—sit down,' said Ana, staring worriedly at Liz's pale features.

'I'm fine, really, Ana,' Liz protested, allowing the older woman to propel her carefully into one of the silk-covered armchairs, her head dropping involuntarily back against the elegant upholstery.

'Please drink this—I insist!' Ana said, placing a glass of mellow-coloured liquid in Liz's unresisting hand. 'It is brandy—please, drink!'

'Ugh! That was awful,' Liz exclaimed with a shudder as she swallowed the last drops from the glass. 'But you were right, it has made me feel better.' She smiled reassuringly at the worried housekeeper, but Ana continued to eye her uncertainly.

'I think perhaps I contact Don Francisco. . . .'

'Oh no! No, you mustn't! Please, I'm fine now—like you said, I'm just not accustomed to the heat out here.'

'You are sure you do not wish me to fetch the Señor?'

'Quite, quite sure, thank you, Ana.'

The housekeeper hesitated a moment and then said: 'You wished to speak with me on some other matter. Shall I return later when you are feeling better?'

'No, that won't be necessary now, Ana, I've changed my mind, but I shall need to use the telephone later. Will—er—Don Francisco be out all day?'

'*Si*. You may use his study at any time, *señora*. Now, if

you are sure that you are well I will go to prepare your luncheon. . . .'

'No—please, nothing for me,' Liz said with a quiver of distaste. 'Will no one else be at home for lunch?'

'No, *señora*. Señorita Marisa is lunching with Señora Diego and Don Francisco and Señor Carlos will be occupied with business until much later. But you must eat something, *señora*, otherwise you will undoubtedly be ill. I shall bring something light to your room,' Ana said with decision, 'and then when you have used the telephone I think you should rest.'

'Perhaps you are right, Ana,' Liz agreed. In truth the peace and security of her own room appealed strongly to her, and she determined that she would follow Ana's advice.

Later in her own room Liz stretched her length on her luxurious mattress, unable to sleep, going over once again in her mind the content of her telephone call to John. She had hated having to deceive him, knowing that when she finally returned home she would have to hurt him further. Whatever Francisco's reasons for inviting her to Riera they had been fatal in so far as the relationship between John and herself was concerned. She could never marry him knowing that she was still in love with Francisco.

With the benefit of hindsight she wished desperately that she had never come to Spain. She was in no doubt that she could have made John happy—but as things stood now, all their lives had been thrown off course. She rolled angrily on to her back and stared unseeingly at the white-painted ceiling. Not only were her own plans ruined, but she had a dreadful suspicion that Francisco was making a disastrous mistake, choosing Luisa for his next wife.

She was forced to admit that her opinions were heavily biased against the woman, but even so, Francisco needed someone to encourage the warmer side of his nature. Someone to laugh with him, someone who would respond fully to his lovemaking. . . . At this point in her musings

Liz groaned softly and deliberately thrust such disruptive thoughts aside. No one could accuse Luisa Rodriguez of being tender-hearted, nor did Liz think that for all her Latin blood she was capable of much passion.

Wearily she stretched her length on the bed. Such conjecture was futile and she knew it. Francisco was surely old enough to know what he was doing, and he was hardly likely to listen to her opinion in any case. . . .

The disturbed night must have affected Liz more than she had realised, for when she awoke it was late afternoon, but she felt no compelling urge to leave the comfort and security of the luxurious bed. Instead she continued to lie indolently in its confines, feeling lethargic and depressed, unwilling to face any member of the Ramirez family after the events of the previous night.

Inevitably the time for dinner approached, and she showered and dressed wearily, trying to still the feeling of panic which threatened to overwhelm her. How could she face Francisco after the things Luisa had told her this morning? Knowing that her actions were causing him a great deal of amusement—it was an impossible situation!

She began to apply her make-up skilfully, attempting to hide the emotional ravages wrought earlier in the day. Her appearance would pass muster, she decided after a critical scrutiny of her reflection in the dressing table mirror. It was true that her eyes were lacklustre and her complexion pale and strained, but a little eye-shadow and blusher had worked wonders, and Francisco was not going to get the opportunity for a close inspection this evening, she determined. Or any other time, for that matter. Theirs must be a strictly business arrangement in the future.

In the event her anxieties were unfounded. She and Marisa were alone at dinner, Carlos and Francisco were both away visiting friends. Liz assumed that Francisco would be with Luisa and wondered with a pang of dismay how much the Spanish woman would tell him about the events of the morning . . . would he hear of her obvious distress at Luisa's disclosures?

But no, Liz couldn't imagine that Francisco would appreciate having his plans thwarted, and if Luisa believed that she had persuaded her to leave early that would presumably be sufficient reward in itself. Even with this comforting thought Liz was a poor companion at dinner. Marisa was very understanding and tactful and did her best to distract her from her own thoughts by keeping up a steady flow of undemanding conversation.

They were just relaxing over coffee in the family *salón* when the outer door banged loudly and there were sounds of masculine footsteps walking across the hall. Liz felt her pulses racing alarmingly and she knew that hot colour had flooded her cheeks, only to fade again leaving her paler than before. She trembled inwardly, knowing that if she were to have such violent reactions every time she had to meet Francisco it would be impossible to get through the next few days.

As the door to the *salón* opened Liz gave an almost audible gasp of relief. It was Carlos who had entered the room, banging the door behind him with little regard for the sensitive eardrums of the other occupants.

'Must you do that?' Marisa placed her hands in mock horror over her ears. 'We have been having a very peaceful evening!'

'Not like yesterday, eh?' said Carlos, with a sidelong glance at Liz's flushed features.

'Carlos!'

'Sorry, Marisa,' he shrugged philosophically. 'But it did happen, and we can hardly pretend to be in ignorance.' After a moment's pause he added, 'I understand that Diego is threatening to sue Francisco for assault.'

'No!' Liz gasped, turning horrified eyes towards Carlos. 'Is that true? Oh, God, what have I done?' To the dismay of Carlos and Marisa Lizbeth's badly shattered self-control finally snapped and she broke ignominiously into tears, burying her face in hands that trembled alarmingly.

'*Dios*, Lizbeth, I am sorry!' Carlos sank on to his knees in front of her, attempting to take her hands into his own.

'Is it really true, Carlos?'

'*Si ... si*, it is the truth! But do not worry, Lizbeth, Francisco is very well able to take care of that ... that. ...' He bit off an expletive with an obvious effort, and continued: 'Forgive me, but I wish that he was here at this moment and I also could hit him.' He ground his teeth angrily, his handsome face distorted by his fierce emotions.

'But what does he say that Francisco has done?' Liz persisted, clutching urgently at Carlos's arm.

'He has broken many of Diego's teeth, and damaged his nose. But that is not very bad,' Carlos said with a dismissive shrug. 'Also he has black eyes. He will not be in a position to force his attentions upon any woman in the near future.'

'Is ... is that what Francisco told you?'

'*Si*. Is it not the truth?'

'Yes—yes, it is true,' Liz agreed, wiping away the tears which still lay on her cheeks with the back of her hand. She shrugged wearily. 'You must admit that I was partly to blame. I didn't exactly discourage his attentions.'

'It is true that you were not altogether ... wise in your treatment of Miguel,' Marisa interposed. 'But in Spain no gentleman would dream of attempting to make love to another man's wife in such circumstances. In the past this would have meant years of enmity between the two families. Miguel would have been fortunate to have escaped with a few broken teeth,' she added, with an uncharacteristic lack of sympathy.

'Oh, God—you and Juan! I never thought ... is he very angry? Miguel is his cousin. ...'

'Yes, that is true, and Juan is angry, but with Miguel and no one else. His parents are a little distressed. Miguel's father is Señor Diego's brother,' Marisa explained carefully. 'But their anger will pass and it will not affect the future of Juan and myself in any way ... do not worry, Lizbeth.'

'I can't help being worried,' Liz said, chewing her lower lip agitatedly, and rising to her feet she began to pace about the room in obvious distress.

'Hey, calm down!' interposed Carlos, placing himself in her path and propelling her firmly back on to the comfortable couch and flopping unceremoniously down beside her.

'Yes ... but what can Francisco do? If he really has damaged Miguel's face surely the man has a case against him?'

'I do not think he would be able to make a case against Francisco,' said Carlos in calm tones. 'Francisco's face was also damaged ... and there were others who saw it. In the circumstances what can he do? Do not worry, Lizbeth, there will be no difficulty.'

Distractedly Liz rubbed her hand across her forehead, which had begun to throb alarmingly in the last few minutes. 'I hope you are right in your assumptions, Carlos. ... Look, will you think I'm very rude if I go to bed? I've developed rather a headache.'

'But of course not!' Carlos rose abruptly from his lounging position beside her. 'I will ring for Ana and ask her to get you some medication ...'

'No, please don't. All I need is rest.'

'I was hoping that you would accompany Marisa and myself to Seville tomorrow, to do some sightseeing, but if you are not well. ...' Carlos said uncertainly.

'As I said, it's only a headache—truly,' Liz reiterated with a faint smile. 'I would love to come if you'll have me.'

After her goodnights had been said she walked slowly up the stairs to her own room, thinking with relief that tomorrow would be another day which she could spend away from Francisco's disturbing presence; and after all, she did want to do some sightseeing in Seville. . . .

Perhaps as a result of her rest earlier in the day she found sleep difficult to attain. In addition to her problems with Francisco, the separation from Edward was beginning to play on her nerves. A brief telephone conversation was no substitute for his actual presence. He had sounded disappointed at lunchtime when she had told him that she was to stay in Spain for the rest of the week. Perhaps she had made the wrong decision once again, she thought, tossing fitfully from side to side, and if Francisco decided to continue his actions of the previous night, would she be able to remain in control? She had begun to doubt the fact when his possible entry into the same room could have such an alarming effect on her.

The throbbing in her head had reached massive proportions and wearily she reached for the light switch, flinching as the glow invaded her temples, causing her to scramble out of bed and head for the bathroom cabinet. Frantically she searched through the shelves; there were numerous bottles of perfume, talcum powder, even insect repellant and sun lotions, but she was finally forced to admit that there were no painkillers of any description.

Belatedly she remembered putting a few foil-wrapped tablets in her purse before the journey, and she had never used them. She closed the cabinet door and returned to her bedroom, opening the nearest wardrobe door. After a few moments searching she realised that her bag was not where it should be. She was beginning to feel faintly giddy now, as the pain from her headache intensified. With a groan of dismay she sank back on to the bed. She remembered now that she had left her bag in the lounge. Carlos's disturbing news had made her forget to bring it.

'Damn! Damn! Damn!' The thought of venturing into the silent house in search of her lost handbag was hardly guaranteed to appeal to her. Without any real hope she closed her eyes, knowing that it was only a matter of time before she succumbed to the violence of the pain and ventured out of her room.

Inevitably the tension in her head increased and she had to accept the inevitable. Throwing on a cool nylon wrapper, she took a deep breath and opened her bedroom door. The upper floor of the *estancia* was reassuringly illuminated by the moonlight flooding through the windows.

On stealthy feet she began to descend the stairs, but when she reached the hall she saw with dismay that the corridor leading to the family *salón* and thence to Francisco's study and the domestic quarters was in deep shadow, and she had the distinct feeling that someone or something was lurking there watching her.

Angry with herself for allowing her disordered emotions so much rein, she drew a deep if rather ragged breath and walked determinedly in the direction of the *salón*, frowning fiercely as the throbbing in her head intensified with the tension of the last few moments.

'Aah!' Liz gave a barely suppressed scream as a hand gripped her shoulder and Francisco's voice demanded:

'Why are you here at this time of night?'

'Don't ever do that to me again!' she said in trembling tones, leaning her head weakly against the heavy panels of the *salón* door.

'I am sorry if I startled you,' Francisco said in a cold voice. 'But, as I said before, why are you downstairs now, when everyone else is in bed?'

'I'm not about to steal the family silver, if that's what you're thinking!' Liz said bitterly, her hackles rising as she faced Francisco's arrogant and unsympathetic figure, her earlier distress at the problems she had caused for him evaporating in the light of cold reality. Certainly there was no trace in his harsh, world-weary features of the emotions unleashed the previous evening.

Liz realised that she had been hoping that Luisa Rodriguez's assessment of the situation was a biased one, but in the face of Francisco's barely concealed dislike she was forced to admit that her hopes had been unrealistic ones.

'I have a headache, and my handbag, complete with painkillers, is in here. Now, do you mind if I get it? Or are you going to continue this catechism all night?' Abruptly she shrugged away his detaining hand and went into the moonlit room, her slender body provocatively outlined beneath its flimsy covering.

Eagerly she picked up her handbag from where she had left it beside the coffee table, very much aware that Francisco had not moved from his position by the door and was regarding her intently from his heavily lidded eyes.

He was not formally dressed at the moment. He was in fact still wearing riding clothes, she noticed, the blue linen shirt rolled up at the sleeves to reveal the dark muscularity of his forearms. Her heart lurched uncomfortably and she forced herself to look away from his still figure.

'Can I go now? You won't want to search me, I presume,' she said in mocking tones as he continued to block her exit from the lounge.

'Don't tempt me, Lizbeth!' he said harshly, and Liz felt her legs begin to tremble alarmingly as she realised that her words could be misconstrued as a direct invitation. Hastily she tried to push past his still figure, only to find her wrist firmly held between his fingers.

'Oh, don't worry, Lizbeth! I am not going to take you up on your very generous offer!'

'Why, you ... you conceited pig!' Liz raised her free hand and would have slapped him fiercely on the cheek, had he not grabbed it with his own. He held her struggling figure for a moment without apparent effort, his expression unreadable in the dim light of the corridor.

'You can stop struggling! As I have said, you have nothing to fear from me.' He shrugged his broad shoulders indolently and leaned his powerful body against the wall, seemingly unperturbed by Liz's angry expression. 'I have a proposition to put to you. It would seem sensible to call a truce between us for the remainder of your stay in Spain. I have to visit the coast on business tomorrow—I thought perhaps you would care to accompany me. It would give you the chance to see a little more of my country. . . . We could ask Marisa too, if the thought' of my undiluted company is too much for you.'

'It's . . . it's kind of you to ask, Francisco,' Liz stammered awkwardly. 'I would have liked to come, but I've already promised Carlos and Marisa that I would go with them to Seville tomorrow.'

'So, then that is settled.' Francisco released her imprisoned hands abruptly, straightening from his position against the wall in one fluid movement.

'Perhaps . . . perhaps we could go later in the week,' Liz suggested tentatively.

'I think not! I have many business matters to attend to . . . but do not let me detain you any longer, Lizbeth! I expect Carlos intends leaving early in the morning. . . .'

'Look, Francisco, I would have liked to come, honestly!' Liz said, her anger against him fading rapidly. Appealingly she placed her hand on his arm and felt him stiffen imperceptibly at her touch.

'You will have to excuse me.' Francisco withdrew his arm firmly away from her touch and moved pointedly towards the stairs. 'I also have to rise early in the morning. I think we should both get some sleep.'

CHAPTER EIGHT

Liz fell asleep surprisingly quickly when she returned to her room, and consequently she awoke in a more cheerful frame of mind, feeling more ready to face whatever the day should bring. It was only eight-fifteen, and she breathed a sigh of relief that she had not overslept once more. As usual the sun was shining brilliantly through the windows, the glare muted and softened by the slatted blinds at the windows.

She showered and dried herself slowly, savouring the luxury of her surroundings, knowing that she could have been deliriously happy here had things worked out differently nine years ago. She sighed, her mood dampened a little by the direction of her thoughts, and as she flicked quickly through her small store of dresses she reflected that she could have been dressing to accompany Francisco on his trip to the coast.

She shook her head in self-derision, thrusting away the disruptive thoughts and forcing herself to concentrate on the task in hand. Finally she selected a simple, sleeveless dress in a becoming shade of blue from the wardrobe and slipped it over her slim figure. With the addition of a light coating of mascara and lipstick and her hair in a quickly assembled knot she felt ready to face the household. It was, after all, much more sensible to be going into Seville with Carlos and Marisa, she reassured herself; and it would give her the added opportunity of being able to buy a present for Edward.

The breakfast room was reassuringly empty, although her relief at not seeing Francisco was combined with a certain amount of regret—at least in his presence she felt fully alive, even though he caused her such distress.

She was finishing her second cup of coffee when Carlos entered the room; a distinctly sullen expression marring his attractive features.

'What is it, Carlos? Has something happened? Is—is Miguel Diego causing more trouble?' Liz felt her heart plummet as she considered the possibilities of Diego's actions. The exchange of personalities with Francisco had served to put it out of her mind—now Carlos's presence had renewed all her worries.

'No, nothing like that,' said Carlos with a dismissive gesture.

'The way I feel at the moment it would be no more than Francisco deserves.'

'Why, what is it?' Liz asked urgently. 'Tell me, Carlos, please!'

'My dear brother has forbidden me to take you to Seville today. He does not think it would be suitable!' He rose jerkily from the chair in which he had been lounging and poured himself a cup of coffee, draining it in one angry gesture and turning to stare broodingly out into the inner courtyard.

'But why, Carlos? Marisa is accompanying us! What possible objection can he have?'

'That's just it! Marisa won't be coming—she has tooth-ache this morning and will have to visit the dentist.'

'I'm sorry Marisa is not well,' Liz said with genuine regret. 'But I still don't see why we shouldn't go to Seville,' she added, feeling a growing sense of anger at Francisco's high-handed conduct. 'We're not his servants, after all . . . we don't have to do everything he tells us!'

'You will have the chance to tell him so in a moment, he is on his way across the courtyard now,' said Carlos. 'I am willing to stick out for this trip to Seville if you will back me up.'

'Don't worry! I don't care to have my decisions made for me,' she said with false bravado, endeavouring to master the flood of warmth which suffused her body at the sight of Francisco's familiar figure.

'Carlos has told you that your visit to Seville must be cancelled for today?' he said abruptly, regarding Liz arrogantly from his heavily lidded eyes. 'I will make arrangements to take you later in the week,' he continued, obviously not expecting any opposition to his decision.

'That won't be necessary, thank you, Francisco,' Liz said quietly. 'I know how busy you are at the moment—I don't mind going to Seville without Marisa and neither does Carlos. . . .'

'But I do!' Francisco ground out harshly. 'There will be no more talk of this visit. You may accompany me to the coast instead,' he told her with characteristic arrogance. 'I can postpone my business commitments on one occasion without difficulty.'

'As I said, that won't be necessary.' Liz smouldered inwardly. How dared he speak to her as though she were a two-year-old without a sensible thought in her head? She had made her own decisions for the last nine years and she was not going to stop now.

She wiped her mouth on the napkin provided and rose steadily from the table, mustering all her composure to face the angry figure in front of her. Whatever his business plans for today they couldn't be very important ones, she concluded, surveying his overpowering figure from beneath lowered lids. Either that or he still had to change for the journey. In brown cord trousers and a cream open-necked shirt, Liz could have wished that he was a less disturbingly attractive figure. She shivered inwardly and said:

'Carlos and I have decided to go to Seville, and nothing you can say will change our minds.' Liz's voice was deceptively steady, although she felt a tremor of fear run through her body when she saw Francisco's face darken with anger.

'Carlos! You will leave us, please. I have things to discuss with my wife.'

Francisco sent his smouldering glance towards Carlos,

and for a moment Liz thought the younger man would obey his brother's command.

'As Liz says, we are going to Seville,' Carlos said flatly.

'There is no harm in it, Francisco. After all, we are brother and sister.'

'Nevertheless I do not wish it! If you persist in this action you must be prepared to take the consequences!' Francisco's brows were drawn together threateningly as he sought by a sheer effort of will to intimidate the younger man. Liz thought the two men had never looked so alike, as Carlos glared unrepentantly at Francisco, his face tight with barely suppressed fury.

'We are going, Francisco! As I have said, there can be no harm in the visit . . . Come, Lizbeth,' he added, placing a protective hand under her elbow. 'We had better make a start before the day gets too warm. Get your things. . . .'

'One moment, Carlos!' Francisco restrained his brother as he would have followed Liz from the room: 'I intend to speak to you further.'

'As you wish!' Carlos replied coldly, with a significant glance at Francisco's restraining hand on his arm. 'I will meet you in ten minutes in the hall, Lizbeth.'

'That will be fine,' Liz said quietly, glancing reluctantly at the still figure of her husband in the open doorway of the breakfast room, feeling an unwarranted surge of sympathy for his silent figure. It was totally ridiculous to feel sorry for Francisco, she told herself firmly as she made her way to her room. The haggard look on his face was merely a result of the shadows in the doorway. . . . When had Francisco ever needed anyone's sympathy?

Quickly she collected a chunky cardigan and checked the contents of her handbag, clipping a few wayward strands of hair securely into the severe knot which revealed the feminine curves of her cheek to perfection. After checking her final appearance in the full-length mirror, she moved swiftly down the steps, beginning to wonder whether perhaps Francisco had persuaded

Carlos to cancel their outing after all.

She licked her dry lips and looked tentatively towards the breakfast room door, half expecting Francisco's brooding figure to appear. When the hall remained re-assuringly empty, she pushed open the outer doors and stood hesitantly on the upper steps, only to smile with relief as Carlos brought a racy-looking sports car to an abrupt halt at the bottom of the steps.

As Carlos climbed out Liz descended the steps quickly, glancing nervously towards the house, half expecting Francisco's angry figure to appear at any moment. She smiled her thanks to Carlos as he held the door for her to slide into the car, watching in mounting trepidation as he walked quickly around the car and slid silently into the driver's seat. He slammed the door with an ear splitting bang, released the handbrake and roared away from the *estancia* with a powerful squeal of tyres, jerking Liz back against the seat with a jarring thud.

'Hey, steady on, Carlos! I'm not tired of life just yet, you know.' She glanced at his angry expression and added, 'You'd better tell me what Francisco has said to you! Maybe it will relieve your feelings a little.'

'*Dios*, I am sorry, Lizbeth!' He slowed the car to a more sedate pace, giving Liz an apologetic glance as he added, 'You are correct in your assumption, of course. It was Francisco who made me angry. Always he treats me as though I am a fool!' he said harshly, with an angry shrug of his broad shoulders.

'Join the club, Carlos!' Liz said bitterly. 'Your brother is an arrogant, bossy, chauvinistic . . . pig, and he always will be! He can't bear to think that anyone is capable of making a decision without consulting him. I only hope for his sake that Luisa Rodriguez has a more amenable personality than I have, otherwise his second marriage won't be any more successful than his first.'

'Francisco has told you that he intends to marry Luisa Rodriguez?' Carlos said quickly, his attention momentarily diverted from his own anger.

'No, not in so many words.' Liz gave a resigned shrug and added, 'It's obvious isn't it? They seem to spend most of their free time together, and it's what both families want, I imagine. You still haven't told me what Francisco said to you,' she added in an attempt to divert the conversation from the painful recollection of Luisa Rodriguez' confidences.

'He seemed to believe that I am not capable of looking after you! Do I seem like a child to you, Lizbeth?' Carlos gave an angry shrug obviously not expecting an answer to his question. 'I intended that we should have dinner in Seville, there are many good restaurants. But no, it is not safe to drive back after dark. Have I not done this very thing many times without incident? However, he will not listen to reason. Will you please light me a cigarette, Lizbeth?' he said jerkily, handing her the packet from an inside pocket of his jacket and indicating the lighter on the dashboard.

'Maybe this will help to calm my temper,' he said, drawing deeply and inhaling with obvious pleasure on the cigarette that she handed to him. 'By the way, Francisco sent that.' He indicated the broad-brimmed straw hat lying in the luggage space. 'He borrowed it from Marisa for you. It is true,' he added reluctantly, 'that I had not thought of this, and you would find shopping very uncomfortable without it.'

'It was kind of Francisco to think of it,' said Liz in constrained tones. She was forced to concede that notwithstanding the chauvinistic character of much of his behaviour, his care for her physical comfort had always been irreproachable. She forced her thoughts away from the pleasanter aspects of his character, and said:

'Look, can we just forget Francisco for now, Carlos? Otherwise it will just cast a damper on the rest of the day, and that would be playing into his hands, don't you think?'

'*Si*, we will not mention him again. Have you decided

where you would like to go in Seville—or would you like to leave the details to me?'

'We-ell, I would like to buy a few gifts while we're there, and definitely I must visit the Alcazar and gardens.'

'Shopping!' Carlos rolled his eyes in horror. 'Why did I not follow Francisco's advice and stay at home, or we could have gone to the Cota Donana instead. There are no shops there,' he added, with a wicked twinkle in Liz's direction.

'You can stop worrying, Carlos,' Liz said with a laugh. 'I shan't spend much time shopping, I want to see as much of Seville as I can, there may not be another opportunity. . . . The Cota Donana that you mentioned—isn't that the wildlife sanctuary?'

'Mm, as you say . . . it is not far from the *estancia*.'

'Would you be able to get a permit, Carlos? I would like to go there if I could, before I have to go home.'

'Yes, of course! Francisco is a regular visitor,' Carlos added surprisingly. 'There would be no difficulty in obtaining permission for a visit. I confess I am surprised at your interest. I would not have thought that crouching in a hot and sticky hide for hours on end was really your—how do you say—scene!'

'I gather the idea doesn't appeal to you?' Liz said drily.

'It is true I am not a devotee like Francisco; but for you, anything!' he said gallantly, smiling warmly at her.

Liz returned the smile, but privately determined not to mention the subject again. There would not be a great deal of pleasure to be gained from such a visit with an uninterested companion. It would have been pleasant, under different circumstances, to go with Francisco, she conceded. He had always displayed an intense interest in natural history . . . but there was little point in thinking about it. She certainly hadn't any intention of asking Francisco to take her!

The journey into Seville passed quickly in Carlos's undemanding company and he parked with casual expertise in the teeming city, steering her towards the most suitable shops without difficulty.

He agreed to wait for her under the awning of an elegant café, with a cooling drink for company, so that Liz felt able to look around the shops without too many qualms. She had already decided that to buy local gifts for Marisa and Carlos would be foolish. She would send them something from England, perhaps a painting of her beautiful, bleak Northern hills. As for Francisco, she somehow doubted whether he would appreciate a gift from her, so that she only had Edward and John to consider.

On impulse she decided to buy a rather expensive but beautifully decorated riding whip for Edward. The choice for John was more difficult in the circumstances. He would probably throw it back in her face when she told him that the wedding arrangements would have to be cancelled. After some deliberation she chose a pair of gloves and a wallet in leather, both exquisitely crafted and very expensive.

Placing her purchases carefully in her capacious handbag, she walked quickly back towards the café, enjoying Carlos's surprised expression at her unexpectedly early return.

'All my adult life I have been searching for a woman who could accomplish a shopping trip so speedily. Perhaps when you have divorced Francisco you would consider a proposal from me, eh?'

He grinned wickedly at her, but raised his arms in alarm as she picked up his half finished drink and threatened him with it.

'Pax! I apologise,' he said on a laughing breath, blissfully unconscious of the interested glances from nearby tables. 'Do you want a drink, or shall we get on?'

'Let's go, Carlos, please,' Liz said with reddened cheeks as she became aware that they were the focus of all eyes.

'To the Alcazar first, yes—you are agreeable?'

'That sounds fine,' said Liz, following him quickly on to the street.

'We should just about finish looking around the Alcazar in time for lunch. I know a delightful restaurant in Santa Cruz which serves the best tortillas in Spain!'

The Alcazar and gardens were very beautiful, and Liz was enchanted despite the overwhelming heat. She was forced to acknowledge that had Francisco not sent the hat she would have found sightseeing unbearable. Their delicious lunch was all that Carlos had promised and they began their sightseeing of the Santa Cruz quarter of the city in a very cheerful frame of mind. Its winding byways and the windows covered with iron grilles evoked centuries long past, and they were soon totally absorbed in its bewitching atmosphere.

However, when they finally returned to the car Liz felt unutterably weary. She gave silent thanks to Francisco for preventing them from staying in Seville for dinner; she thought of a refreshing shower and her cool shadowed room with longing.

Both she and Carlos were silent on the return journey, but it was a comfortable silence, she acknowledged, without any of the overtones which would have been present in Francisco's company. She yawned involuntarily and stretched luxuriously in her seat.

'You are tired, Lizbeth?'

'Mm, yes, a little. Nothing that a shower and a rest won't cure.'

'As Francisco says, I am a careless fool,' Carlos muttered. 'Will you forgive me, Liz? I had no idea. . . .'

'Don't be an idiot, Carlos! I'm no more tired than if I'd made this trip with Francisco, or anyone else for that matter. . . . We are nearly home, aren't we?' she said, peering through the car windows into the darkening countryside with growing recognition.

'Yes, safe and sound.' Carlos swung the car expertly on to the road to the *estancia*, his horn blaring loudly as a rather moth-eaten dog ran in front of the car from one of the nearby cottages.

Liz found herself thinking of the *estancia* and its environs with familiar warmth. When she had called it home to Carlos earlier it had not been a slip of the tongue. If only things had worked out differently she could have been very happy living here.

'Well, here we are,' Carlos interrupted her musings abruptly, a puzzled note in his voice as he added: 'I wonder what has occurred? Ana seems very anxious to speak with us.'

'Señora Ramirez! Oh, Señora Ramirez! Thank goodness you have arrived at last! Come at once to the telephone, please, you are wanted urgently. They have been trying to contact you for the past two hours.'

Liz felt suddenly sick with fear and grasped the top of the car to support her unsteady legs.

'Has something happened to Francisco, has he had an accident?'

She saw Carlos looking at her strangely, but just at that moment she did not care what construction was put upon her actions. Concern for Francisco had driven out any other consideration.

'No, no hurry, please! It is a call from England. A close relative who is ill, I understand.'

With a frantic burst of speed Liz rushed into Francisco's study. It must be Edward who was ill. Dear God! It must be Edward. Praying desperately that Ana was mistaken, Liz lifted the receiver with hands that trembled wildly.

'Hello, hello! Oh, John, it's you! What's happened— what's happened?'

'Liz, get back here as soon as you can, do you hear me? Don't wait to pack or anything, get a flight immediately! Edward was rushed into hospital with violent abdominal pains about two hours ago—they think his appendix may have burst!' he added harshly.

'Is he—will he—recover?' Liz gasped, all colour draining from her face as she pictured her son, lying defenceless and alone in a strange hospital while she was in Spain and unable to comfort him in any way.

'They're very hopeful Liz, Liz! Are you there?' The silence stretched interminably as Liz fought to regain control of her emotions.

'Yes, yes, I'm here. . . . Where is Edward, John? Which hospital?'

'St Mary's. Come straight here—I will be waiting for you, and remember, I love you, darling.'

'I know that, John—I'll be with you just as soon as I can, goodbye.'

She replaced the receiver with hands that still trembled alarmingly and subsided gratefully into the chair which Carlos brought towards her; accepting, almost without being aware of it, the generous measure of brandy which he also provided.

'Your son is ill?'

'Yes—yes! I have to get home! I shouldn't be sitting here like this,' she said, struggling to her feet, gripped by an overwhelming feeling of panic.

'Two more minutes will not make any difference,' Carlos stated, propelling her firmly back into the armchair. 'I will deal with the bookings for your flight home, while Ana fetches you some food and arranges for your bags to be packed. There is little point in doing anything further until we have ascertained the times of flights to England.'

'It's the holiday season—what if there are no vacancies at such short notice?' said Liz, despair evident in her voice.

'There will be no problem,' Carlos replied confidently, and it was clear to Liz at moments like this that his likeness to Francisco was not only physical.

The next twenty minutes were a nightmare. Liz was gripped by the most terrible forebodings, and she knew that she would find it hard to forgive herself for not being by her son's side when he needed her.

She was tormented by doubts about her past actions. The events of the past week had made it abundantly clear to her that if only for Edward's sake she ought to have swallowed her pride and forced Francisco to accept the truth of his son's paternity. It had been wrong to deny Francisco the son he so desperately wanted, and she admitted to herself that he would have made an excellent father. Even though Carlos sometimes resented Francisco's high-handed manner, it was obvious that he, like the rest of the family, was devoted to Francisco.

In many ways Liz was thankful that Francisco was not at home at this time. She knew that she would willingly have allowed him to take complete control of the situation, Placing absolute reliance upon his firm strength the temptation to unburden herself completely and explain the truth about Edward would have been immense, but to do so at this time would be needlessly cruel. She would just have to bear the burden on her own shoulders. When Edward began to recover would be the time to tell Francisco the truth.

She ate the food which Ana provided, mechanically, not tasting the luscious prawn-filled omelette or the warm, fragrant rolls that accompanied it. She was drinking her second cup of coffee when Carlos entered the room and she felt that the meal had made her more ready to face the future.

'There is a flight from Seville in just over an hour. Don't worry, we will make it!' Carlos told her, laying a restraining hand on her arm as she began to scramble to her feet.

'You have the cases packed, Ana?' Carlos asked, turning to the housekeeper for confirmation.

'*Si, señor.*'

'That is good! See that Rafael puts everything into the car, please. Now, we are almost ready. Here is your passport, Liz, and a jacket for your journey. I think we have everything now?'

'I don't know how to thank you, Carlos,' said Liz, fighting to restrain the tears which filled her eyes.

'Save it! You will have the opportunity later. I am coming with you to Madrid and all the way to England if necessary,' he said firmly in a tone which brooked no argument.

He propelled her to the door, his arm reassuringly strong around her waist. Ana was waiting, a solemn expression on her normally cheerful countenance.

'Goodbye, Ana,' said Liz. 'Thank you for taking such good care of me.'

'It has been a pleasure, *señora. Hasta la vista!*'

Carlos opened the door of the sports car and Liz sank on to the seat.

'Marisa! My God, Carlos, I haven't said goodbye!'

'Calm down,' he said quietly, climbing into the driving seat. 'She went with Francisco to Madrid to see the dentist there. They are staying with our mother tonight. Don't worry Liz I have left a note for Francisco explaining everything—we shall not have time to contact them from Madrid airport as your connecting flight will have to be made very quickly.'

He turned the key in the ignition and the powerful engine roared into life.

'Relax, Liz, and try to get some sleep. It will be an uncomfortable ride, I am afraid, I must drive quickly if we are to catch the flight—but I will be careful, do not worry!'

In normal circumstances Liz would have been completely terrified on that wild journey, but although on occasions her heart leaped into her mouth with fear, for the most part she found herself silently urging Carlos to greater speed, visions of Edward in his hospital bed overriding all other considerations.

The airport terminal of San Paulo was brightly illuminated and bustling with travellers, and Liz felt completely disorientated and confused, but Carlos steered her competently through the formalities, taking charge of her cases and settling them both on the plane with minutes to spare.

Liz leaned her head against the seat and closed her eyes thankfully, too concerned about Edward to worry about the take-off or the rest of the flight. She viewed the remainder of the journey through the haze of a nightmare, the only reality herself and Carlos—the other passengers figures from another world, speaking and moving but totally without importance to her.

Their arrival at Madrid was completed without difficulty, and once again she allowed Carlos to take complete charge without demur. She quelled the fleeting urge to telephone Francisco and pour out her troubles on to his broad shoulders. She had made the final decision to bring Edward up alone and now she must face the consequences. Time enough to contact him when Edward began to improve, and if he then wanted to take her son away from her, she was forced to acknowledge that he had a certain amount of justice on his side. Indeed, providing that Edward recovered she was willing to agree to almost anything to ensure her son's happiness.

She followed Carlos to the departure point for the plane to England, making no effort to discourage him from accompanying her, and only when they finally reached England did she begin to function again. The cool drizzle and biting wind was a shock after the overwhelming heat of Andalucia and she had reason to be grateful for Carlos's thoughtfulness in providing her with a coat.

They had some time to wait for a connection to Yeadon, and Liz put an urgent call through to the hospital for news of Edward. There was a heart-stopping delay before she was able to contact the correct ward, and she licked lips that were dry with fear when a soft Scottish voice answered the telephone.

'Mrs Ramirez?'

'Yes—yes—have you news of my son Edward, please?'

She held her breath, the pulses throbbing alarmingly at her throat as she waited for the reply.

'I have good news for you, Mrs Ramirez—he has had his operation and the trouble was not as bad as we first thought. He's still under anaesthetic, but there's no reason why he shouldn't make a swift recovery.'

Liz expelled her breath slowly and leaned her head for support against the mirror in the telephone booth. Her legs felt too weak to support her weight, but she managed to speak shakily into the receiver.

'He's going to get well—you're sure?'

'There's no reason to think otherwise, Mrs Ramirez,' the disembodied voice replied gently. 'I understand you're out of the country?'

'We—we've just landed at Heathrow. I'm hoping to reach the hospital later today.'

'That's wonderful! Edward will just be coming round. It will be a wonderful surprise for him . . . will his father be with you?'

'Er—no—no, possibly his uncle. My husband will be arriving later. I must go now . . . the plane, you understand.' Liz no longer felt able to continue the conversation, a combination of relief at Edward's improved condition and worry about Francisco made words difficult to form. 'Goodbye, and thank you, thank you so much.' She replaced the receiver with a click and stumbled out of the box, straight into Carlos's comforting arms.

'It is bad news, *querida*?' he asked softly, his accent thickened with distress.

'No—oh no, Carlos!' Liz looked at him with eyes brimming with tears. 'He's going to get well. I'm only crying because I'm so happy.'

The hot tears overflowed and coursed freely down her cheeks. She fumbled for a moment in her bag, accepting Carlos's proffered handkerchief gratefully.

'Can we go somewhere to talk, Carlos?' she said, her

voice still unsteady with suppressed emotion. 'Do we have time . . . before the flight, I mean?'

'But yes, we shall have to cool our heels for another hour and a half. The restaurant should be fairly quiet at this time of day, and I must admit that I feel quite hungry,' Carlos added, rubbing his stomach ruefully.

'Carlos, I'm so sorry!' Liz exclaimed in anguished tones. 'I never thought! While I was eating you were making arrangements for the journey. I really am a selfish pig.'

He shrugged his broad shoulders expressively. 'I could have eaten on the plane had I wished, but I confess that I was too concerned about you to feel hungry. Now—well, now I shall enjoy my meal.'

He smiled at her and hustled her into the clean, impersonal restaurant, settling her courteously in her seat, his dark good looks attracting more than one feminine glance, Liz noticed. She herself felt an immense sense of relaxation, the extreme pallor had gone from her cheeks and she felt more able to think of other things, now that the worst of her worries about Edward were stilled.

She was free to tell Francisco the truth about Edward, and that decision made, another great burden had lifted from her shoulders. Whatever the consequences she felt she was following the right course of action at last.

She experienced a tremor of fear when she pondered Francisco's reaction to the news. If he had wanted to gain his revenge on her in the past, how much greater his reasons would be now. Although there was a certain irony in the fact that previously he had hated her for apparently giving birth to another man's child, and now he would hate her because the child had been his.

She squared her shoulders mentally, determining not to accept all the blame for the situation herself. Francisco had been pigheaded and arrogant and had never even begun to trust her. He had immediately jumped to totally wrong conclusions, and if she had not sought to alter those conclusions at the time—well, he would no doubt be very ready to blame her, but perhaps others would not.

She accepted a second cup of coffee thoughtfully, pleased that his preoccupation with a plate of beef salad had given her time to collect her thoughts. She watched him devour a piece of lemon meringue pie, with an inward shudder. She still felt nauseous at the thought of food, her stomach she felt sure would reject anything other than liquid.

'Mm, that's better.' Carlos leaned back with a sigh of satisfaction. 'Do you mind if I smoke, Lizbeth?'

'No, go ahead, please.'

She watched quietly as he extracted a cigarette from his silver case, searched for a moment in his jacket pocket for his lighter and ignited the tip, drawing with obvious enjoyment on the object.

'You wanted to tell me something, Lizbeth?'

'What? Yes—oh yes. Sorry, Carlos, I was miles away.' She hesitated a moment and then said, 'I don't really know how to begin—you're not going to like this, I'm afraid,' she added after a moment, twisting the leather strap of her bag between hands that had begun to tremble nervously.

'Go ahead anyway, Lizbeth. It can't be such bad news, surely?' he said, a puzzled expression on his handsome features.

Taking a deep breath, Liz said without preamble: 'Edward is Francisco's son, not Andrew Mellor's—or any other mythical lover's, for that matter.'

She saw Carlos's face darken with bewilderment.

'I do not understand, how can this be?'

'There's no doubt, Carlos—you'll be in no doubt when you've seen Edward, he's very like both Francisco and yourself.'

'*Madre de Dios*, Lizbeth! What can I say to you? Why have you done this . . . how could you?' Carlos stared at her in shocked amazement and Liz lowered her eyes momentarily before the accusation in his own, only to raise them again as she said bitterly:

'Perhaps you should say those words to Francisco and not to me. I never said that Edward was not Francisco's son . . . it was all in Francisco's imagination. I didn't have a lover, Carlos—I never wanted anyone but Francisco,' she added, shaking her head bitterly.

'He never really loved me or trusted me, what was I to do . . . plead with a man who'd shown quite clearly that he thought me a tramp? What if Edward hadn't looked like a Ramirez—eh?' She met Carlos's shocked expression bravely, speaking more fiercely now as memories of that painful time swam to the surface of her brain. 'He would still have been Francisco's son, but I doubt whether he would have been completely accepted.' She broke off. 'Look, do you have a cigarette to spare?'

'I thought you didn't smoke?'

'I don't, but I need a cigarette now if I'm not to disgrace us both by bursting into tears.' Liz indicated the occupants of the surrounding tables, more than one of whom was watching the progress of their impassioned conversation with interest.

'What are you going to do?' Carlos lit her cigarette with a hand that trembled slightly, but his voice was calm as he added:

'Are you going to tell Francisco about the boy?'

'Yes—yes—I must, of course,' Liz drew jerkily on the cigarette, her eyes watering as the unaccustomed smoke wreathed around her face.

Carlos sighed a little desperately. 'I do not need to tell you that there will be trouble!'

He rubbed his eyes with both hands—a curiously weary gesture. 'I will do all that I can to help you.' After a moment he added: 'That does not mean that I agree with your actions—to deprive Francisco of his heir was cruel, but that you were the victim of considerable provocation, yes, that I will concede. It would seem that where you are concerned Francisco's habitually good judgment is warped by jealousy.'

'Is that what you call it?'

'*Si!* Even now, after all these years of separation he cannot bear to see you—how shall I say—associating with any other man. I assure you he was considerably disturbed when you insisted upon accompanying me to Seville.'

Liz raised her eyebrows in disbelief. 'Don't get the wrong idea, Carlos! He still considers me as one of his possessions, that's all. There are no warmer emotions involved, I promise you.'

'You seem very sure.' Carlos shot her a look from under lowered brows and began rather abstractedly to toy with the ashtray. 'I think you could be mistaken.'

'I thought so too at one time,' Liz sighed, grinding out her smouldering cigarette with jerky movements. 'Luisa Rodriguez soon put me right on that score.'

'What do you mean? What can she know?'

'Oh, what's the use? You may as well know the whole story, Carlos. It's pretty sordid,' she added, with a bitter twist to her lips. 'Did you know that Francisco's ostensible reason for inviting me to Spain was to persuade me to cancel the divorce proceedings?' Liz glanced enquiringly at Carlos and was rewarded by a nod of agreement.

'*Si*, he did tell me this, and surely this fact alone would point to a continuing interest?'

'Oh God, if only you knew!' Liz laughed self-derisively. 'He told me himself that he had no interest in me as a woman—although I did have some reason to doubt that statement at a later date,' she added with heightened colour.

'I can imagine,' Carlos interjected drily.

'I even began to hope . . .' she broke off hurriedly, 'but that's by the way. The important fact is that I had a visit from Luisa Rodriguez—the morning after the dinner party, actually.'

'Francisco and I were at the vineyard and Marisa was with Juan—I remember.'

'Mm—well, she came to speak to me, for my own good,' Liz added with a wry laugh. 'She said there was something I should know about Francisco's plans for the future.' She paused for a moment and endeavoured to steady her emotions, amazed that Luisa Rodriguez's words should still have the power to hurt her.

'It would seem that Francisco's plans for continuing our marriage were complete pretence.' She shrugged her slim shoulders wearily. 'It was his intention to make me fall in love with him again, then he would have divorced me himself and married Luisa Rodriguez.'

'She told you that?' Carlos exclaimed in amazement.

'Yes!'

'And you believed her?'

'Is there any reason why I shouldn't have? Francisco certainly seemed to be very interested in Luisa,' said Liz in a bitter voice. 'And his behaviour was odd from the moment I arrived. One minute he appeared to hate everything about me and the next—well, he was wanting to make love to me. It hardly follows, does it?'

'You were not exactly—conciliatory—yourself, and yet I assume that you were willing to respond to his lovemaking. Does that mean that you had a similar scheme in mind?'

Liz lowered her eyes before Carlos's direct gaze. 'I wasn't going to placate him, Carlos ... not when he was so beastly to me. Oh yes, I'll admit that I enjoyed his lovemaking and I would have been prepared to be—friendly—at other times, if only he'd been willing to meet me half way.'

'And what of John?'

'John?' Liz gazed blankly at Carlos.

'The man you are going to marry ... or had you forgotten?'

Liz let out her breath on a shuddering sigh. 'I had forgotten—you were right. I can't marry him now ... I shall have to tell him today when we reach the hospital.'

Carlos shot her a glance. 'Francisco succeeded, then?'

'What do you mean?'

He raised his shoulders expressively. 'You are still in love with him, are you not?'

Liz's heart was pounding so heavily that she felt sure that everyone in the restaurant would be able to hear it. 'You must promise never to tell Francisco, please! I couldn't bear it if he knew.' Bright tears sparkled unshed in her eyes as she added: 'He and Luisa would find it very amusing.'

'You need not worry that I shall ever give Francisco a reason to laugh at you, little sister,' said Carlos, placing his hand over her own cold one where it lay on the formica surface. 'But come, we must catch our flight. Time enough to decide on your future course of action when we have seen Edward.'

CHAPTER NINE

THE persistent cold drizzle had stopped and the sun had begun to shine when they reached Yeadon airport. Liz knew that she ought to have phoned John from London and then he would have come to collect them, but somehow she shrank from meeting him in Carlos's presence, having to maintain the polite façade of their relationship until she had time to speak to him alone. She found herself wishing that he would not be at the hospital—now that Edward was improving he would surely have returned home.

The taxi they hired made good time through the silent streets. The morning traffic was only just beginning to flow as they purred to a halt close to the main entrance of the hospital. Carlos paid the driver, and Liz had cause to bless his foresight once again, as apart from loose change she was completely without English money.

They entered the reception area and were directed to a ward on the second floor. There was still no sign of John and Liz began to hope that that was one unpleasant task which she could put aside until later.

The buxom Irish Sister who met them outside Edward's ward confirmed John's departure. He had left a message asking Liz to contact him at home as soon as possible.

'And now you would like to see your son, I expect, Mrs. Ramirez?'

'Please, if that would be possible.'

'This is Mr Ramirez?'

'Well—yes and no. Mr Ramirez is Edward's uncle.'

'Your husband will be coming later, I expect?'

Liz felt her colour rising rapidly as she encountered the woman's faintly puzzled expression. She began to wonder what explanation John had given for his presence and she was immensely grateful when Carlos replied for her.

'My brother is away on business at the moment, he will perhaps arrive later today—and now may we see my nephew? Mrs Ramirez is anxious. . . .'

'Of course, please come this way.'

Liz found herself marvelling at the effectiveness of that unconscious air of arrogance and command which both brothers possessed in full measure; all difficulties had been eradicated immediately. The ward was a long open one, old-fashioned but clean and airy; with polished floors and flowers in rather ungainly groups on every available windowsill.

Edward's bed was halfway down the ward, on the left, and Liz and Carlos had to run the gauntlet of numerous pairs of interested eyes before reaching Edward. In normal circumstances she would have been overcome by pity for the pale and listless children who peered at them from some of the beds, but today all her attention was given to the motionless figure of her son, lying with closed eyes in a patch of watery sunshine.

'Is he all right?' She turned anxious eyes to the Sister in charge, only to be reassured by her next words.

'Of course, don't worry—he's doing very well, but he's still tired from the operation and the anaesthetic. There are some chairs at the end of the ward if Mr Ramirez would like to fetch them, then you could sit here quietly until he wakens,' she said kindly. 'I must leave you now, but if you should want me I'll be in my office.'

'Yes, thank you very much, Sister.' Liz smiled gratefully at the nurse and then sat stiffly in the chair that Carlos placed for her beside Edward's bed.

'As you say, there can be no doubt about his paternity,' Carlos murmured in subdued tones. 'He is the image of my brother.'

Liz shot him a look. 'Did you doubt it, Carlos?' and then after a moment she said, 'He's very pale. I wish I'd never left him. Do you think he really is going to get well?'

'Calm down, Lizbeth, you heard the nurse, he is doing very well.'

They waited quietly beside Edward's sleeping figure for what seemed to Liz to be an age. There was a steady buzz of chatter from the other occupants of the ward, interrupted now and then by louder noises from the livelier occupants, but eventually faint traces of movement drew their attention to Edward, and they watched silently as he began to move uncomfortably on the pillows.

'Edward!' Liz grasped his restless hand firmly, 'Edward! it's Mum, are you feeling better, love?'

'Mm . . . .' Wearily the heavy lids lifted and for a moment the large brown eyes, so like Francisco's, stared blankly into her own. 'Mum! Mum, where am I? What's happened?' As Edward struggled into a sitting position both Liz and Carlos pushed him firmly back on to the pillows.

'You're O.K., love, but you must keep still,' Liz said, more calmly than she felt.

'Why are you crying, Mum?'

'I'm just so pleased to see you, Edward,' she explained, as she wiped the tears from her cheeks with the back of her hand. 'We've been so worried about you. You were taken ill, don't you remember?'

'The pain! Yes, I do. Ooh, Mum, it was awful!' Edward told her, screwing up his face in remembered agony. 'Where's Uncle John?' he asked suddenly, 'and who is this?' He fixed Carlos with a disconcertingly direct gaze. 'You must be a relative of my father's,' he said, after a moment. 'You look quite like me, don't you?' he added frankly.

'That is so, Edward. I am your father's brother.'

'Why haven't you been to see us before? Don't you like us?'

Liz felt the colour draining from her cheeks. 'I don't

think this is the time for explanations, Edward. You've been very ill and you must put all your energy into getting well.' She squeezed his hand reassuringly. 'I can promise you some nice surprises when you're feeling better—so hurry up and get well! In any case, it was my fault and not your uncle's that you haven't met before. . . . I've told you, there'll be plenty of time for explanations later,' she said more firmly, as Edward appeared intent upon pursuing the subject. 'Just get well first, if you please!'

'Do you think you could bully the nurses instead of me, Mum, and get me something to eat? I'm starving,' Edward murmured with a faint grin.

'I might be able to manage that!' Liz smiled with relief as she walked through the ward to the Sister's office. Edward must be on the mend if he had regained his appetite already. The Sister reassured her that breakfast had not yet been served and would be sent to the ward in about fifteen minutes, and Liz returned to Edward's bed to hear Carlos describing vividly some of the horses in Francisco's stable.

'Hey, Mum! Uncle Carlos says if I visit him in Spain, he'll teach me to ride. Isn't that great?' Excitement had brought a flush of colour to Edward's cheeks and a sparkle to his eyes; but his next words caused Liz's own colour to drain rapidly, leaving her pale and shaken.

'He says his brother owns the whole estate and the horses. Is he my uncle too, Mum?'

'I told you, explanations later, Edward,' she said, more sharply than she had intended. 'Please don't get Edward so excited, Carlos. It can't be good for him. Breakfast will only be a few minutes, Edward, but in future I'll have to bring some sandwiches and things into the ward. I don't expect the nurses will be able to give you anything to eat between official mealtimes.'

'O.K., Mum, thanks,' Edward murmured in subdued tones.

'I'm sorry I snapped at you both, love. It's just reaction,

I guess. . . . If you promise not to get excited your uncle can talk about horses as much as he wants, right?'

'I'm very much afraid there won't be time at the moment. You are coming to tell us that we must leave now, isn't that so, Sister?' Carlos rose courteously to his feet as the nurse approached.

'I'm afraid so, Mr Ramirez,' and as Liz would have protested she added: 'We're flexible about visiting in the children's wards, but we don't normally admit parents so early in the day, and also Edward needs to sleep. I think you should leave him for the rest of the morning and come to visit him again—say, any time after lunch.'

'Yes . . . yes, as you wish, it was kind of you to admit us so early.' Liz tried to keep her voice steady, knowing that any distress on her part would only upset Edward in his present weakened condition. She bent to kiss him gently, squeezing his warm brown hand as it lay on the white coverlet. 'I'll be back this afternoon, love. Be good, won't you?'

'Mmm, O.K., Mum, but you will be back, won't you?'

'Of course your mother will come back, Edward,' the Sister interposed firmly. 'You'll be so busy this morning, seeing doctors and being pestered for your temperature and blood pressure, that you won't have time to miss her. Go now, Mrs Ramirez—Edward will be fine, I promise you.' She smiled reassuringly at Liz. 'You can both come back this afternoon, if you like.'

'Yes, thank you, we will. Let me know if there's any change, please. You have my home number?'

'Yes—and don't worry. This young man is going to be fine. He'll be playing football again in no time.'

'Yes—well, goodbye, Edward, I'll see you later.'

'G'bye, Mum! Don't forget to come after lunch. 'Bye, Uncle Carlos, will you come too?'

'Yes, I will see you later.'

Liz hurried unseeingly from the ward, aware of a certain sense of relief that at least some of the questions concerning Carlos and his brother must wait until later, when, she hoped, she would have had time to sort out her own chaotic thoughts. When she was considering the question of disclosing Edward's paternity, all her worries had been concerned with Francisco's reaction. She had never previously considered how Edward would react. That he might eventually choose to live in luxury with his father—yes, she had been prepared to accept that possibility, but that he might come to hate her for depriving him of a family for so many years was a contingency that she was only just beginning to appreciate.

She forced herself to put such thoughts aside for the moment. Edward would obviously not have to be told about his father at this early stage. Later perhaps, when he was stronger.

She was distracted from her musings by Carlos's firm hand in the small of her back, propelling her towards a taxi, which had just delivered an elderly woman to the outpatients' department. In the ensuing bustle Liz was forced to concentrate upon present circumstances—giving the driver directions and attempting to persuade Carlos to stay with her, instead of at a hotel.

'It will be much better if I take a room at a hotel,' Carlos insisted. 'Your reputation, you understand . . . and also if Francisco should come. . . .'

'Why should he? Did you leave a message asking him to?'

'No. But I think he will wish to come,' Carlos said with a faint shrug.

'Well, even so, I hardly think he'll want to stay with me.'

'No,' Carlos agreed quietly, 'but you will want privacy—both of you. There will undoubtedly be matters to discuss . . .'

'Oh, undoubtedly,' Liz said bitterly, 'and believe me, I don't blame you for wanting to be as far away as possible.'

'That is not the reason and you know it! If my presence would help in any way I would be there; but in the circumstances it will only make matters worse. I know Francisco, and believe me, you will be better alone, Liz.'

'If you say so.' She shrugged. 'You will come back to the hospital this afternoon with me, won't you? Edward will expect you.'

'Yes. Don't worry so much, Liz.' He patted her arm reassuringly. 'Francisco will no doubt be very angry at first, but his pleasure in Edward will soon alter that. When I have dropped you at home I will go into the town and buy myself some essentials,' he added, 'a toothbrush and a raincoat, perhaps.'

'I'm so sorry Carlos, I never thought about your lack of luggage. Do you have sufficient money? I could go to the bank.'

'No, please do not bother.' He dismissed her worries with a casual gesture. 'If Francisco does not come I shall have funds transferred. There will be no problems.'

When Liz reached home she found herself unable to settle She went immediately next door to reassure Mrs Helliwell about Edward's condition. She refused her offer of breakfast and went into her own empty house once more, trying not to think that this was how it would be if Edward left her and went to live with his father in Spain.

She fidgeted in the kitchen, putting on the kettle and making a welcome cup of tea, knowing that eventually she would have to telephone John and let him know she had arrived home.

Her hands were trembling when she finally picked up the receiver and dialled his number. The phone rang for an interminable length of time and Liz realised belatedly that he would probably still be in bed, after staying late at the hospital the previous evening, but her stomach gave a sickening lurch as the receiver at the other end was lifted.

'John Spencer here, who's speaking, please?'

'John, it's me, Liz!'

'Liz darling, forgive me—I've only just woken—I should have expected. . . .'

'I'm sorry I woke you, John, I should have waited until later.'

'It doesn't matter,' he said quickly, brushing her excuses to one side. 'What's wrong, Liz? Is it Edward? They said last night that he was doing well and they haven't rung, so I assumed. . . .'

'It's not Edward—he's doing well. I've seen him this morning and he's fully conscious. I have to go back this afternoon. But you're right, John, there is something I have to tell you.' She hesitated, uncertain how to broach the subject. 'I should wait and tell you face to face, I know that—but I have to do it now . . . I have to tell you now. I can't marry you, John.' Suddenly and brutally Liz said the cruel words. 'You were right, I never should have gone to Spain.' She gave a gasping sob into the waiting silence. 'I still love Francisco. . . . I should never have gone!'

'I see.' His voice sounded cool, detached almost as he added, 'You won't be getting a divorce, then.' After a moment, 'Have you told him about Edward?'

'No, I haven't told him yet, I shall have to do that soon. I don't know about the divorce. Francisco's feelings haven't changed, and I'm not intending to live with him again.'

She sensed the hope beginning to grow in his voice. 'In that case let's not do anything hasty, Liz. Leave it for now, later when you've had time to think.'

'No!' She almost shouted the word into the receiver. 'I can't, it won't work, John—believe me, if I thought there was a chance I'd take it.'

'I see. You really are hooked aren't you? Well, I suppose it's better to find out now than after the wedding, but don't expect me to take it in a gentlemanly fashion,

Liz. If I ever meet that Spanish husband of yours I shall be strongly tempted to take a whip to him.'

Before Liz could reply, John's telephone was firmly replaced on its cradle and all she could hear was the empty buzz of the dialling tone. She felt drained of all energy and flung herself on to the plump cushions of the couch, unable to assimilate any new emotions in her crowded consciousness.

She must have slept, because it was the insistent ringing of the doorbell that roused her. She glanced quickly at her watch—it was turned eleven o'clock, so she had slept for two hours, but it was not yet time for Carlos to collect her to go back to the hospital.

She went to the door, a vague sense of disquiet lingering in her brain, to be confronted by the dark, forbidding figure of her husband.

'Francisco! No . . . oh no!'

'But yes, Lizbeth, are you not going to invite me into your home, mm? I think that you must do so, *querida*. What I have to say to you cannot be said on the public thoroughfare, I assure you.'

The expression on his face was almost satanic in its anger, his eyes blazing in his otherwise cold, still features, the lines at the side of his mouth etched in deeply by his suppressed fury. Liz removed her trembling hands from her face and stood aside passively, allowing Francisco to walk past her into the cheerful but rather shabby room.

'So this is where my son lives? You have made some changes since you lived here with your parents.'

'Yes.' Her voice was totally without inflection, she felt dead, her spirit completely crushed by the contempt and hatred in his eyes.

'It is not exactly . . . luxurious, but that should make him appreciate his inheritance in Spain more keenly.'

'You . . . mean to take him?'

'What did you expect? That I would leave him here with you?' he said contemptuously.

'We've been very happy here, together.' Her voice broke ignominiously on the words and she turned away from his arrogant figure, seeking to control her shaken emotions.

'Spare me the tears, Lizbeth,' he ground out harshly. 'You think I can feel sympathy for you after what I have just discovered?'

'You went to the hospital straight from the airport, I suppose?'

'As you say,' he replied grimly. 'I asked if my wife, Mrs Ramirez, was still in the building. They said no, but practically insisted that I should visit my son.' He shrugged explicitly. 'It seemed easier to comply in the circumstances.'

'It was of course a natural assumption on their part, that any child of mine would be my husband's too,' Liz said bitterly, turning once again to face her husband, some of her precarious composure regained. For a moment her words seemed to pierce his anger and she surprised a momentary flicker of doubt.

'They also assumed that a father and son would know of each other's existence,' he said coldly.

'Edward! Oh God, Edward! What have you told him? Has it made him ill again?' In her agitation she approached Francisco and gripped his arms fiercely, shaking him with all her strength.

'I have done nothing to Edward. He has been told, but has taken it calmly,' he added, momentarily disconcerted by her onslaught.

'You're certain? Oh, what's the use—I must ring the hospital—where have I put the telephone directory?' Liz began to search frantically through the books on the lower shelves, pulling them out wildly on to the floor in her urgency.

'Leave it! Leave it, I said!' Francisco reiterated more firmly, giving Lizbeth's shoulders a small shake. 'They promised to telephone me here if there should be any change, and we are due back at the hospital anyway in,' he glanced briefly at his watch, 'two hours.'

'What did Edward say?' Liz asked in trembling tones.

'He refused to believe the nurses at first, but then, when he saw me, he was not difficult to convince. It would seem that he has already met an unknown uncle today . . . a resurrected father did not seem so difficult to accept under the circumstances,' he added with a shrug.

'Did you stay to talk to him?'

'For a few minutes only. They were concerned that he should rest. He is still very weak.' After a moment he added, 'I have arranged to see the consultant this afternoon when we return. I wish to have Edward transferred to the private wing.'

'You had no right. . . .'

'I have every right, Lizbeth, and it is time that you understand the matter. The boy bears my name, and I assume that I am named as the father on the birth certificate?' He broke off a moment and drew a silver cigarette case from his jacket pocket, extracting a tipped cigarette and lighting it in a leisurely fashion. Liz sank wearily into a convenient chair, no longer able to maintain the pretence of composure.

'You know your name is on the birth certificate,' she said in muffled tones, 'I informed your solicitor.'

'So you did . . . and very convenient it will prove to be should you try to interfere in any arrangements concerning the boy.'

'You'll stop at nothing to get your own way, will you?' Liz raised anguished eyes to his own harsh face and Francisco shot her a look, his expression softening imperceptibly as he noticed for the first time the haunted look in her eyes and the drawn pallor of her cheeks. He turned away and drew luxuriously on his cigarette, saying after a moment's pause:

'Do you have anything to eat in the house?'

Liz gazed blankly at him. 'I'm sorry, what did you say?'

'Food! Do you have any food in the house? I have not eaten for some time.' He glanced quickly at his watch. 'Otherwise I will have to find a restaurant before we return to the hospital.'

'There's no need, I can make an omelette if that will do, I haven't eaten myself since I arrived home.' She rose a little wearily from her seat and walked towards the kitchen. 'We'll have to eat in the kitchen, I'm afraid.'

'No matter. Is there something I can do?'

'No, nothing. I won't be long. I don't have much food in the house, only what the next-door neighbour has bought for me.'

'Your parents, they do not live here now? They have moved elsewhere?'

Liz gazed in surprise at him for a moment, and then said:

'They're dead. They're both dead. I thought you knew.'

'No, no—I am sorry!' His face mirrored his concern. 'I assumed that they were helping you with the boy when you would not accept an allowance.' He followed Liz into the cheerfully decorated kitchen and gazed blankly out of the window at the well kept lawn and vegetable garden, fronting the windswept hills of the surrounding moors.

'Why did you not accept the money I offered then, mm? Particularly as the boy is mine. Perhaps that is the reason . . . because Edward is my son you were using him to demonstrate your hatred of me more strongly.'

Liz went through the motions of preparing the meal automatically, all her attention focussed on Francisco and his disturbing words.

'I don't hate you, Francisco,' she said eventually, in a voice devoid of all emotion. 'Not now, anyway. I did hate you at first, that's true, but really I refused your money because I was proud. You ought to to be able to understand that, Francisco. It's surely a familiar emotion to you.'

He turned to watch her as she placed bread and condiments on the table and then moved to attend to the percolator, from which an enticing smell was already emanating.

'Did Mellor leave you when he saw the child and realised that it was mine? he asked abruptly. 'You could still have contacted me—it wasn't too late.'

'You never will understand, will you, Francisco?' Liz sighed wearily, pouring the frothing eggs into the hot butter with half her attention. 'It doesn't matter whatever I do or say, you'll always think the worst of me. There never was any doubt about the father of my child! I've never allowed any other man to make love to me!'

'You allowed me to think that the child was Mellor's!'

'No, you're wrong, Francisco! I told you I was going to have a child, it was your assumption that the child had been fathered by some other man. You'd better eat this before it goes cold,' she added prosaically, placing the appetising plateful on to the melamine surface. Francisco lowered himself on to a kitchen chair, appearing completely alien in those domestic surroundings.

'You made no attempt to correct my false assumption.'

'Should I have done so? I'd already pleaded my innocence—you refused to listen to me.' Liz shook her head wearily. 'What was I supposed to do? Crawl on my knees to you?'

'Why did you leave the flat?' he asked abruptly.

'What do you mean?'

'Can you deny that you disappeared, left the flat without providing any means of contacting you? You went with Mellor then, didn't you, Lizbeth? Can you deny it?' Francisco said harshly.

'Oh, what's the use of my denying anything to you, Francisco?' Liz cried. 'I was convicted and sentenced years ago. Eat your omelette, it's going cold. I think we'd better continue our discussion of Edward's future through our solicitors.'

For a few moments there was complete silence in the room as Francisco attacked the food on his plate with frowning concentration.

'That was delicious, Lizbeth, you are a good cook! What is the matter?' he added, glancing at her barely eaten meal. 'Aren't you hungry?'

'No, no, I can't eat it,' said Liz with a small shudder of distaste. 'It must be worry about Edward. I shall feel better when he's completely out of danger.'

'I think that you are also worrying about the future ... We shall settle matters here and now, before we leave for the hospital,' said Francisco, in a voice which brooked no argument. 'But first you will tell me why you left the flat!'

'No, Francisco, please! I don't want to talk about it ... not now.' Liz leaned her elbows on the table and supported her forehead with hands that trembled slightly.

'Yes, now! Where did you go if not to Mellor?' Francisco continued inexorably.

'I came here ... to Yorkshire, but surely you must have discovered that fact from the solicitor?'

He inclined his head arrogantly. 'That is so, but there was a gap of some weeks between you leaving the flat and contacting the solicitor. ... I want to know where you were during that time!'

'The housekeeper contacted you, I suppose?' Liz rubbed weary fingers over her eyes and added, 'I can't remember now whether I saw her to explain why I was leaving or not.'

'It was not the housekeeper.' Francisco leaned back in his chair and stared fixedly at her for a long moment. 'Is there any more coffee?' he said abruptly.

'Yes ... yes, of course. I'm sorry, I should have asked you. ...' Liz stammered, momentarily disconcerted by the change of subject.

After drinking his coffee quietly for a moment, he said:

'I returned to the flat after you had left.'

'Did you? I hadn't realised, I presumed you would send for your things later.'

'I did not return for my belongings, Lizbeth.'

'Then why? I don't understand.' Liz raised her eyes to encounter his disturbingly direct stare and lowered her glance beneath the look in his own.

'I think you understand very well.'

'I don't believe you—you're just trying to make me feel even more guilty . . . you hadn't the smallest intention of returning to resume our marriage—and even if you had,' she added, rather incoherently, 'I've done nothing to be ashamed of.'

She pushed her chair away from the table and began rather haphazardly, to collect the dirty dishes, piling them with a clatter on to the working surface beside the sink. Perhaps the familiar actions helped to soothe her a little, because as she filled the bowl with water and detergent she began to speak more calmly.

'I received a telegram a day . . . two days after you left . . . I can't remember exactly.' She wrinkled her brow in concentration and then shook her head dismissively. 'It doesn't matter anyway. The telegram was to tell me that Mum and Dad had been in a car accident, and I had to come directly to Yorkshire . . . to the hospital.'

She glanced towards Francisco before continuing, but he was seemingly absorbed in the glowing tip of his cigarette. 'When I reached the hospital, Dad had already died. Mum . . . Mum lived for a couple of days after the accident.' She shrugged her slim shoulders wearily. 'Afterwards I didn't have the energy to do anything. In fact I don't think I could have coped at all without the help of Mrs Helliwell from next door. Particularly not when I discovered that I was pregnant on top of everything else.

'Fortunately Dad left enough money for me to live on until Edward was old enough to go to nursery school for a few hours a day. I took a secretarial course while I was pregnant,' she explained quietly, 'and I managed to find a job as a school secretary when I was free to work. It fitted in well with Edward's hours at school . . . and Mrs Helliwell looked after him if ever I was late.'

'This is the truth, Lizbeth?' Francisco said harshly, grinding his cigarette into the ashtray with controlled violence.

'Yes, it's the truth.'

'I can check the story, of course.'

Liz shrugged wordlessly. 'Oh, what's the use, Francisco . . . what does it matter now? It's all past and done with and you'll never change your opinion of me, whether you check the story or not. Surely the only important thing now is Edward's future.'

Francisco stirred uneasily in his chair. 'Whatever the truth of your story, it does not alter the fact that you kept our son away from me for nine years.'

'No!' Liz protested. 'It was you! Your solicitor wrote and said you didn't want to receive any further communication about the child, if you remember?'

'What was I to think?' Francisco said harshly. 'What would any man have thought? I returned from Spain to find you in Mellor's arms and then later, when I came back to the flat, it was to discover that you had packed and left without a word. . . . When you wrote to me to tell me about the child, naturally I assumed that Mellor was the father.'

At these words Liz's frail hold on her temper finally snapped and she was unable to restrain her feelings any longer.

'You make me sick, Francisco Ramirez!' she screamed with unaccustomed violence. 'How dare you come here, pushing your way into my home with your accusations and threats? You're a brutal, unfeeling beast!' she continued, well launched on her theme now that the floodgates were finally opened, all the despair and anger which she had bottled up inside her for years pouring into the open.

'You must be blind, Francisco!' she continued. 'I think you must be blind!' She gave a gesture which encompassed the whole of the small house with its shabby furniture. 'Do you truly believe I'd be living here with my son if I were the gold-digger you take me for? Am I so unattractive that you think I couldn't have persuaded some other wealthy man to marry me if I'd wanted it that way?'

Tears of rage had begun to stream down her face and her voice had thickened with the emotion of the moment. 'I only accepted your ... your bribe to visit Spain for Edward's sake. I hoped the money would perhaps help to make life easier for him as he grew older.

'Do you really think I enjoy going out to work and leaving another woman to care for my son? Do you? I love my son, Francisco! But then you don't know anything about love, do you? You pretend you've loved and been deceived on two occasions, but in reality you're talking about lust ... and hurt pride. Love involves trust, and wanting the best for the other person.

'You even arranged a marriage for Marisa without knowing the first thing about her wishes. Oh yes,' Liz continued fiercely as Francisco would have interrupted, 'fortunately for her she's in love with Juan, but would it really have mattered to you if she hadn't been? Like I said, Francisco, you don't know the first thing about Marisa. Did you know she would have liked to study archaeology at university, eh?' she continued relentlessly. 'No, of course you didn't, because you never thought of asking what her wishes were, did you?'

Francisco raised his hands in a gesture of helplessness, his face pale beneath its accustomed tan, but Liz continued her attack without mercy.

'Fortunately for Marisa Juan is a considerate man, he's asked about her hopes for the future and she tells me that he's willing for her to continue her studies after they're married, if that's what she wants. . . . She's more fortunate than I was . . . Juan will stand by her when she needs him. Where were you when I needed you, Francisco? Where were you when Mum and Dad had their accident and when I had to go into hospital to have the baby? If you'd cared anything at all about me, you would have tried to help then, whether you believed the baby was yours or not.

'Oh what's the use? You're a selfish swine and always will be,' she gulped, turning away from him to wipe away the tears which continued to pour down her cheeks. 'Naturally you assumed that Andrew Mellor was Edward's father! Everyone else assumed that you were the father, but you had other ideas. I think that says it all, don't you?' Liz finished wearily, all her passion spent. 'I think you'd better go now, Francisco. I don't suppose this is doing either of us any good.'

'Damn you! No good at all. For the past nine years my hatred of you has helped to guard against any other emotion.' Francisco rose abruptly and walked slowly to the window, the deep lines on his face thrown into sharp relief by the midday sunshine. 'Then you asked for a divorce and suddenly you were back again in my life. I wanted nothing so much as to make you suffer as I had suffered. I asked you to Spain so that you would be unable to obtain a divorce. I intended to say that we had resumed our marital relationship. No court would have given you a divorce in the face of such evidence,' he said bleakly. 'Then we met again and all my preconceived ideas meant nothing. You were more beautiful than ever and I . . . I wanted you . . . but you knew that, did you not, Lizbeth? I made it very plain, I think.'

He began to walk towards her slowly and she retreated until her trembling legs were pressed against the kitchen cupboards.

'Don't, Francisco! Not now, please!'

He shook his head wordlessly in disgust at his own vulnerability.

'Whatever you have or have not done, Lizbeth, I want you! I think I shall always want you,' he groaned softly, allowing his mouth to burn a trail of fire from her delicate ear to the trembling corner of her vulnerable mouth.

'No, no!' Liz pushed fiercely against his resisting body, drawing her head away from the weakening attraction of his caresses.

'You want me too, Lizbeth! You think that I can hold you in my arms like this and not know that you feel exactly as I do?'

'No!' Liz protested fiercely. 'No, I won't let you do this. You think I'll be more amenable about Edward if you make love to me.'

The grip on her arms slackened and, suddenly she was free.

'Be very sure, Lizbeth, whatever happens I intend to have Edward with me. If you stay here with your ... fiancé ... it will be without Edward. You must make the choice, Lizbeth ... either come back to Spain or lose Edward.'

'What ... what do you mean, come back to Spain?'

'I am willing that you should return to Spain as my wife. Your life will be more restricted than it is here, of course, and I shall expect you to behave in a, shall we say, dignified fashion.'

'I see, and if I don't behave as you expect you'll use Edward as a hostage for my good behaviour. Have you listened to none of the things I've said to you, Francisco?' Liz said bitterly. 'If you expect me to come to Spain under those conditions, you must be mad!'

Francisco made an angry gesture. 'I have to confess that I find you completely infuriating. I came here with a perfectly legitimate reason for being furiously angry with you. I have been here for less than two hours and already I am made to feel the guilty party.' He shrugged his broad shoulders in a resigned gesture. 'I ask you to return to Spain with our son and you see this as some foul plot on my part. It is true,' he added after a moment, 'that I would expect you to be a wife to me in the fullest sense of the word.' He shot her a disturbing look from under his brows. 'But then I have reason to believe that you would not find it so distasteful. . . . Who the devil can that be?' he added, as the harsh ringing of the doorbell disturbed the heavy silence.

'It must be Carlos,' said Liz, hurrying thankfully towards the door. 'Come in, Carlos . . . er . . . Francisco is here.'

'So I see.' Carlos entered the room and gazed enquiringly at his older brother, who was watching him from the kitchen doorway.

'You have seen the boy?' Francisco said abruptly.

'Yes . . . have you?'

'Mm.'

'So—o,' said Carlos on an unsteady breath, glancing from Liz's still figure back to Francisco, 'you know, then?'

'As you say . . . I know.' Francisco paused a moment and levered himself away from the door frame. 'I appreciate your bringing Liz to England; however . . .'

'However, my presence is no longer required,' Carlos interposed in dry tones. 'Don't worry, Francisco, even I can take such a broad hint. I will cancel my hotel room and return home immediately. One of us ought to be on hand at the vineyard at this time.'

'Oh, but Edward expects to see you. . . .'

'I should like to see him again too, Liz, but he will have his father.'

'You will see him. I intend to bring my son to Spain as soon as he is able to travel.'

'I see,' said Carlos, with a sympathetic glance at Lizbeth's vulnerable figure.

Seeing the direction of his brother's gaze Francisco added:

'Lizbeth will return with me also.'

'My God, that's the most sensible thing you've said for years!' exclaimed Carlos, apparently not noticing Liz's small, helpless gesture of denial. He leaned forward to kiss her still face. 'I will be seeing you soon, then, little sister. The taxi is still waiting—I intended to use it to visit the hospital, but if you don't need it, it may as well take me back to the hotel.'

'I rented a car,' Francisco said briefly, accompanying his brother to the door. 'I will keep you informed,' he added, as Carlos climbed into the waiting taxi.

'Yes, let me know how the boy progresses, and ... don't be too angry with her, Francisco. She had reason. . . .'

'I will see you within the next couple of weeks, you can safely leave the problem of my wife to me, Carlos,' Francisco said firmly as the car began to pull away. 'Have a safe journey.'

When Francisco walked back into the house, Liz was standing in front of the mirror, unsuccessfully attempting to secure the silken folds of her hair into a neat roll.

'Oh, damn it, I shall never be ready to go to the hospital at this rate!'

'Leave it loose,' ordered Francisco, from directly behind her. 'I like it.'

With an almost impatient gesture he slid his arms around her, drawing her resisting body firmly back against his own, leaving her in no doubt as to the extent of his desire for her. With a muffled exclamation he buried his face in the rich folds of her hair. His caressing hands sent shivers of flame through her veins, banishing all her resistance. With an obvious effort he moved his body away from hers, his voice unsteady as he said:

'There is no time ... I have arranged to meet the consultant at two o'clock ... *Por Dios*, do not look at me like that, Lizbeth!' he muttered, as she stared at him with eyes still dazed from his lovemaking.

'Later, *querida* ... we must go now. Here are your things, Lizbeth.' He handed her the jacket and bag which she had laid on the chair and propelled her gently towards the door.

It was a silent journey to the hospital, each of them occupied with their own uncertain thoughts. Liz wished with all her heart that she had not seen Luisa Rodriguez before she left Spain. If she had not known of his plans for her, she would have had no hesitation in accepting his invitation to return with him. At least she would have had a few brief weeks of happiness, until Francisco had won Edward's confidence and no longer needed her presence.

Liz sighed inwardly. She would have to visit her own solicitor and find out her legal position. Surely she would have some rights where Edward was concerned? In any event she could not really believe that Francisco would be so cruel as to deprive her completely of her son's presence. Although she realised with a pang of despair that this was exactly what she had done to him during the last nine years.

The visit to the hospital passed more smoothly than Liz had feared. The consultant agreed to transfer Edward to the private wing within the next day or two and she had perforce to be content with Francisco's decision. He was also able to set both their minds at rest about Edward's health and assure them that their son was now on his way to a full recovery.

Edward seemed a little bemused by Francisco's presence, but showed not the slightest sign of blaming Liz for keeping his father's presence a secret for the last nine years. He listened with awed concentration to Francisco's description of life in Spain, obviously absorbing every detail to relate to his friends at a later date.

The afternoon passed quickly, but when the nurses brought the tea trolley into the ward, Liz took the opportunity to slip away and telephone the solicitor. For

the sake of her peace of mind she knew that she would
have to clarify her own position. When Alan Armitage
agreed to meet her that same afternoon she was relieved
rather than otherwise.

Francisco stared at her coldly when she made her
excuses to Edward, but promised to return in the evening.

'Don't worry, Mum, Dad will stay, I'll be fine. He
says we can go to Spain for me to recup . . . recuperate,
that means get better,' he explained carefully. 'No
school for weeks and weeks. Won't that be great,
Mum?'

'We shall have to arrange for you to have tuition at
home, also you will have to learn Spanish,' Francisco said
in amused tones. 'I do not think you need to worry that
you may fall behind with your work, Edward.'

'Ugh! Won't I have any time for riding or exploring,
and things?'

'Yes, when you are fully recovered I shall teach you to
ride myself. Don't worry, we shall maybe allow you a
little free time,' he said with a quiet smile.

'You're teasing me,' Edward said accusingly.

'Maybe . . . now say goodbye to your mother, Edward.'
Then to Liz: 'We shall see you later?'

'Yes, I shan't be long. . . . Would you like a sandwich
or something brought back, or will you go out to the snack
bar later?'

'I will get something when you return. Don't worry,
Lizbeth.'

'See you later, then. Goodbye, Edward,' she murmured,
kissing him gently on the cheek.

' 'Bye, Mum!'

The offices of Binns and Armitage were not situated very
far from the hospital, and Liz walked there with time to
spare before her appointment. The waiting room was
rather bare and comfortless, this being a branch office

and only open on two days a week. She had been fortunate that Alan Armitage was 'in residence' today and not at a more far-flung outpost.

She was forced to admit that managing nowadays without a car was difficult sometimes. At least she would not have that problem if she decided to return to Spain with Francisco. No doubt when he finally rejected her he would be very generous financially.

If only she were the type of person he imagined, how much easier life would be. She could just accept the money offered and go her own way. If she had been willing to swallow her pride she could have accepted Francisco's help at Edward's birth and saved herself a hard struggle into the bargain.

Mr Armitage's secretary interrupted her musings and soon she was comfortably ensconced in a huge armchair, in the rather shabby office. She had not often had reason in recent years to call upon her solicitor's services, but whenever she had done so, had found his placid, rather chubby countenance, and calm good sense infinitely reassuring.

'You have a problem, Mrs Ramirez?' he said, coming straight to the point. 'By the way, do you mind if I smoke?' He indicated a rather battered-looking pipe lying on the ashtray and Liz shook her head.

'No . . . no, of course not.'

He applied a match to the blackened bowl, drawing heavily until the tobacco appeared to be lit. 'Hm, that's better.' He smiled engagingly at Liz. 'My one vice, or so I tell my wife. Now how can I help you?'

'It's really about Edward,' Liz began, 'my son.'

'Yes—just a moment, let me refresh my memory. Some years ago we handled certain correspondence between yourself and your husband concerning the boy. He refused to enter into any further communication regarding the child, I believe?'

'Yes,' Liz nodded jerkily. 'He chose to believe that he

was not Edward's father, but now he's discovered that this was not so and he intends to take Edward back to Spain with him.'

'I see!' Alan Armitage whistled softly, 'I see, indeed. Look, perhaps you'd better start at the beginning, Mrs Ramirez, and put me completely in the picture. Then I shall know exactly where we stand.' He shot her a look. 'I'm assuming that if possible, you want to keep the boy with you?'

Liz raised her hands in a helpless gesture. 'If there's any chance whatsoever. . . .'

'You tell me the complete story and then I can fill you in on your legal position.'

When Liz had finished her story, he lay back for a moment in his chair, probing the bowl of his pipe with a spent match.

'Do I have any legal right to Edward, after denying him to his father for all these years?'

'My dear Mrs Ramirez,' said the solicitor, frowning irritably at his pipe and discarding it on to the already overflowing ashtray, 'the question surely is, does your husband have any right to the boy?'

'But his name is on Edward's birth certificate and I'm still legally married to him. . . .'

'You assure me that you've kept all the communications which you received from your husband at the time of your separation?' As she nodded he continued, 'You kept a copy of the letter which you sent, informing him of the birth of the child and the one he sent in reply, disclaiming any further interest?'

'Yes, but . . .'

'You're about to tell me that you deliberately intended to mislead your husband about the paternity of the child, in the hope that he would leave the boy with you? A perfectly natural action in the circumstances and not one that you ought to worry about at this stage. Legally, in this case, it's the action which you took, rather than any double motive, that would concern the court. I think we can safely say that you would be allowed to keep the boy. However,' he hesitated momentarily, 'it's likely that your husband would be granted access, although I doubt whether he would be allowed to take the boy out of the country.'

'I wouldn't mind that,' said Liz, and then: 'Did you mention court proceedings?'

'Yes, but there again, don't worry about cost. Legal aid should . . .'

'It wasn't that,' Liz interrupted quickly. 'In the circumstances, why are court proceedings necessary at all?'

He shrugged his plump shoulders expressively. 'From everything that you've told me about your husband, it seems unlikely that he'll give in without a fight. Incidentally, I think you also have strong grounds for divorce in this case, if you wish to pursue it. Your position would be much stronger if you were divorced.'

'Yes, I'll think about it.' Liz pushed the subject to one side and said intently, 'If the case went to court, would the papers get hold of it?'

'Oh, no doubt about it . . . have a field day. Oh, don't worry, Mrs Ramirez,' said Alan Armitage as he saw her expression. 'The sympathy would be totally in your favour. Your husband would undoubtedly be the villain of the piece!'

'I see . . . well, thank you for fitting me in this afternoon, Mr Armitage, and thank you for explaining everything so carefully to me.' She rose to her feet, pushing back the chair resolutely.

'Would you like me to contact your husband's solicitor, Mrs Ramirez?' Mr Armitage rose to his feet politely and walked round the desk to shake hands with his client.

'Can you leave it for now? I'll ring you . . . probably tomorrow . . . when I've finally decided what action to take,' she said.

'Very well, I look forward to hearing from you,' he

said, opening the door into the waiting room and escorting
Liz to the street.

After she left the solicitor's office, Liz walked thoughtfully
into the town centre. Absently going into a small coffee
bar, she ordered a salad roll and a cup of rather tasteless,
frothy coffee. By the time she had consumed her snack
and begun the walk back up the hill towards the hospital,
she was no nearer to a solution.

She knew that to expose Francisco to the notoriety of
court proceedings would be unforgivable, and yet she
knew she could never face the alternative solution of seeing
Edward only occasionally, perhaps never. She was reluctantly forced to the conclusion that the only way out of the
difficulty was for herself and Edward to disappear out of
Francisco's life for good—although quite how she would
accomplish the action she was at a loss to decide.

Liz sighed bitterly as she reflected that with a more
reasonable man it would have been sufficient to have
pointed out the facts as the solicitor had put them to her.
But as Alan Armitage, the solicitor, had surmised,
Francisco was a very determined man, and he would fight
every step of the way whatever the cost to himself.

Determinedly she pushed the problem to the back of
her mind for the moment and climbed the hill at a
renewed pace. She must speak to Francisco again about
the subject and find out exactly what he intended. Perhaps
they could reach some reasonable arrangement, she
thought without any real conviction.

She soon reached the imposing Victorian building and
climbed the steps to the main entrance. There were more
visitors in the children's ward when she reached it and
Francisco was still sitting beside Edward's chair, watching
him intently as he lay sound asleep, blissfully unaware of
the noise and chatter around him.

'Ah, Lizbeth!' Francisco rose from his seat by the bed
and came to meet her. Taking her elbow firmly and

drawing her out of the ward into the corridor: 'I want to talk to you.'

'Suppose Edward wakes up?'

'He will assume that I have gone for a meal.' He shot her a glance. 'You have accomplished your business?'

'Yes, yes, thank you. I want to talk to you about it, actually.'

'Spencer is being difficult about your returning to Spain?'

'Spencer? I don't know what you. . . .'

'I assumed that you had been to contact your . . . fiancé,' he interrupted smoothly, 'to tell him about my proposal. That is his name, is it not?'

'Yes, yes, but it wasn't that! I haven't seen John,' Liz stated, carefully not explaining that her relationship with John Spencer had become impossible the moment she had met Francisco again. 'I—I've been to see a solicitor.'

'So—o!' Francisco stiffened momentarily. 'And what did this solicitor have to say?'

'He—he wants me to ask you about—about access. Would you let me see Edward if I didn't come to Spain with you?'

'I have told you,' Francisco said harshly, his face assuming a forbidding aspect, 'if you choose to stay here with that . . . with Spencer, then I shall take Edward away!'

'But surely you would allow me to see him sometimes?' Liz protested tremulously.

'If you chose to come to Spain alone—yes, under those circumstances you could see him, but he will not return to England!'

'Oh, Francisco, you're cruel!' Liz murmured.

'And you are not?' he answered harshly. 'Am I to assume from the tenor of this conversation that you are unwilling to return to Spain as my wife?'

Liz shook her head wordlessly and, turning, rushed down the corridor and out of the swing doors of the entrance. She thought she heard Francisco call her name, but she neither stopped nor turned to look behind her. There was little point in pursuing a conversation which so plainly was not going to accomplish a solution, and had she stayed longer in his presence she would undoubtedly have broken down completely.

It was becoming increasingly obvious that she would have to pursue her plans to disappear, with Edward, from Francisco's life and the sooner she put her mind to wrestling with the difficulties involved, the nearer to a solution she would be.

She managed to retain her self-control during the journey home and was forced to give Mrs. Helliwell an account of Edward's condition before she could reach the sanctuary of her own home. If Francisco and Carlos had been seen and wondered at, Mrs Helliwell was tactful enough not to mention the subject. Nor did she press Liz to stay for tea, merely adjuring her to get in and put her feet up and not worry about Edward, who was obviously as strong as a horse and would be up and about in no time.

Liz rang Edward's ward immediately and was told that he was still asleep and that Francisco was still with him. 'Would you give him a message for me, please, Nurse?'

'Mr Ramirez, you mean?'

'Er—no, Edward . . . when he wakens. Please tell him that I've had to return home—I'm feeling unwell,' she said unsteadily.

'Don't worry, Mrs Ramirez, I'll tell him.'

'Can I visit tomorrow?'

'Yes, any time after nine—Oh, I think Edward is being moved to the other wing in the afternoon, so don't come then. Either come to this ward in the morning or to the other wing in the evening. I think that would be best.'

'Yes, thank you.'

Liz replaced the receiver with a click, then shivering

with reaction she lit the gas fire and went to sit in front of
it. She had not been far wrong when she had told the
nurse that she was ill. The accumulated emotion of the
past two days had made her stomach feel decidedly unsteady. Scratch meals and lack of sleep would not have
helped either, she realised. It was obvious that bed was
the only place for her at the moment, and indeed she
thought with longing of the temporary oblivion that sleep
would bring.

In the event her worries overcame even her extreme
tiredness and she tossed and turned uncomfortably
through the long hours of the night. Eventually giving up
the attempt to snatch any more sleep, she rose in the faint
light of dawn and stumbled down the stairs to the kitchen,
putting on the kettle and pulling back the blinds to let in
the uncertain daylight.

The birds were singing noisily, but the morning was
wrapped in a damp, grey blanket of fog. Liz glanced at
her watch. It was later than she had thought, the grey
light had deceived her. At least it meant that she had less
time to waste before she could visit Edward.

After she had drunk a cup of tea she returned to the
bathroom, running a luxuriously full tub of water and
sprinkling in a handful of bath salts, determinedly relaxing
in the scented depths. She had finally decided upon her
course of future action and immediately her mind felt
easier. She would have to get a job in a large city,
Birmingham perhaps, or Manchester. Not London, she
had decided, because although the chances of bumping
into Francisco there were remote she was unwilling to
leave the smallest thing to chance. Once they got away it
must be a final break.

They would get a small flat to begin with. . . . She had
enough money to tide them over until she could get a
suitable job. Edward would have to go to a child minder
after school, of course, but Liz deliberately closed her
mind to that problem. They would make the move first

and deal with the minor difficulties as they cropped up.

A loud banging on the kitchen door roused her from her somnolent state and she sat up with a jerk, aware that the water had cooled perceptibly. Hastily she climbed out of the bath and began to dry herself vigorously, throwing her housecoat over her faintly damp limbs.

The knocking had stopped when she reached the kitchen door and she peered out tentatively into the garden. The milk was on the step, so it would seem that if the milkman had had a query he had decided to leave it for another day. Carefully she stepped out on to the gravel path, grasping the slippery milk bottles firmly.

'So—you are here.'

'Oh, Francisco! You made me jump. I nearly dropped the milk,' Liz exclaimed, clutching the bottles tightly to her chest, her breath ragged and uneven in her throat.

'I am sorry. I could not make you hear at the front door.'

'No, I—was in the bath.' Liz was suddenly very conscious of the damp and dishevelled state of her hair, and of her bare toes, showing beneath the hem of her housecoat. 'Did . . . did you want something?'

'Yes. May I come in?'

'I'm n-not dressed!' Liz stammered unnecessarily.

'So I see,' Francisco murmured with raised brows. 'Do you think you could make me a cup of your excellent coffee . . . and then we can talk?'

Liz shrugged helplessly. 'I suppose so . . . if you'll just wait until I dress. . . .'

'Surely that won't be necessary! You are adequately covered,' he said, with a glance at her housecoat.

Liz acquiesced silently, but she was overwhelmingly aware of Francisco's alien figure, disrupting the atmosphere in the kitchen as she placed the percolator on the gas ring and set cups, saucers, milk and sugar on to the table.

'Would you like cereal or some toast, or have you eaten?'

'Yes, that sounds good. I confess I could not sleep. I have been thinking ... walking around the town since—well, quite early.' He came to sit at the table and watched Liz intently as she prepared the food. 'Tell me, you have had time to consider my proposal again ... are you still of the same mind?'

'I can't come to Spain with you as conditions are at the moment—you know that!'

'If I said that I would endeavour to control my ... desires ... if I promised not to touch you, would that make you change your mind?'

'It wouldn't make any difference, Francisco.' Liz stared intently at the bubbling coffee pot, carefully avoiding Francisco's eyes.

'So! It is not my attentions to you which you find so distasteful?'

'I don't want to talk about it,' Liz murmured. 'Just leave it, please! But I must warn you,' she added, 'I shall fight to have Edward visit me here ... you won't have everything your own way!'

'Did you keep the correspondence from the early days of our separation?' Francisco asked abruptly.

'Why do you want to know?'

'If you kept those letters then you could easily prevent me from taking Edward to Spain. Legally, that is,' he added in a conversational tone. 'Surely your solicitor told you this?' As Liz remained silent, he continued: 'Why have you decided not to fight me for custody, Lizbeth?'

'Perhaps I haven't.'

'I think so.' Liz heard Francisco yawn and stretch heavily and then she heard the sound of his chair being pushed away from the table, as he rose and walked the short distance towards her averted figure.

'Shall I tell you why you are not going to press the case, hmm?'

Liz felt his hands grip her shoulders gently and said

tremulously, 'You don't know.' Inwardly she began to
feel a rising panic at Francisco's words. Surely he could
not have guessed about her half formed plans to disappear
with Edward? She stiffened as he began to draw her unyielding figure inexorably back against his own.

'Well, let me ask you something else,' he continued,
'When do you intend to marry John Spencer?'

'You said I couldn't get a divorce!' Liz protested
weakly, overwhelmingly conscious of the nearness of the
man she loved so dearly.

'If, for the sake of argument, I agreed to give you a
divorce, what then?'

'I . . . I don't know.'

Abruptly Francisco turned her to face him, grasping
her chin firmly in his hand and staring intently at her
expressive face.

'Let me answer that question myself, Lizbeth. The
answer is never! Do you understand? You are never going
to marry John Spencer. I went to see your erstwhile fiancé
myself yesterday, after I left the hospital. Oh, don't
worry,' he added with a wry grimace, 'he is still in one
piece, there will be no more threatened law-suits to deal
with.

'However, he did have a great deal of interest to tell
me. His comments were brief and to the point, and not
exactly complimentary to my character, believe me,'
Francisco said with feeling. 'After my conversation with
you yesterday I was already very troubled . . . I began to
understand many things which had previously been un-
clear to me. His comments merely served to underline the
stupidity of my past behaviour.'

Abruptly he released his hold on her and went to stare
out of the window at the damp and misty garden. 'I realise
that I was far too ready to doubt you in the early months
of our marriage. I was a fool, Lizbeth, but my experience
with your countrywomen had not encouraged me to
trust.'

He gave an uncertain gesture and continued: 'I believe that subconsciously I always knew that you were not interested in my money. When Carlos first told me that you would not come to Spain to see me, I was angry—very angry. And when he said that he did not believe you were the sort of woman to be interested in a bribe I laughed at him, but secretly I suspect that I hoped it was true. Carlos could not understand why I became even more angry when you finally accepted the money and agreed to come to Spain.

'I realise that it is asking a great deal to expect you to forgive me, Lizbeth. My behaviour has been selfish and cruel in the extreme. My only defence is that the jealousy which I felt where you were concerned ruled out any possibility of a sane reaction.' He shrugged defensively. 'Also your actions at the time were not always designed to set my mind at rest. And Mellor . . . what was I to think when I came home unexpectedly and found you in his arms, hmm? I could have killed him!' he muttered with remembered violence.

He turned and walked towards her once more, placing his hands on her shoulders in a curiously gentle gesture. 'Now do you understand?' he said quietly. 'You are never going to marry Spencer . . . or anyone else. You are mine, do you hear me! You belong only to me and I shall never permit you to leave me again!'

With a fiercely possessive movement he gathered her into his arms, his mouth descending firmly on her own, demanding an instant response from her trembling lips. 'Can you deny that you want me?' he murmured unsteadily after a few nerve-shattering moments.

'No! It is true, I do want you,' Liz said tremulously. 'But I won't come back with you to Spain, Francisco.'

'So! You still believe the story you were told by Luisa Rodriguez, hmm?'

'How did you. . . .'

Francisco raised an unsteady hand and began to

smooth the still damp hair from her brow.

'Carlos told me. I shall have some things to say to Señora Rodriguez when we return to Spain!'

'He—he promised not to say anything.... What else did he tell you?'

Liz raised her eyes to his own and encountered such a look of tenderness and love that she felt hope rising in her breast. Could he look at her in such a way and not feel some warmth towards her? Was it possible that Luisa Rodriguez had not told her the truth?

'What else could he tell me?' Francisco questioned softly, raising a quizzical brow as the warm colour rushed into Liz's cheeks.

'Nothing. I ... are you saying that you didn't invite me to Spain to make me fall in love with you again?' She bent her head so that her hair partially concealed the expression in her eyes, and Francisco reached out a lazy hand and looped a thick swathe around her ear.

'Look at me, Lizbeth!'

'Please, Francisco, answer me,' she begged.

With a groan of impatience he leaned his forehead on to her own. 'It was not my original intention to make you fall in love with me, but I must confess that after a few days ... no, let me be honest,' he said softly, 'after a few moments in your presence it seemed a highly desirable situation.'

Liz began to tremble almost uncontrollably. 'You—you planned it with Luisa Rodriguez?'

'Do not be foolish, *querida*! Have I not just denied that Luisa Rodriguez knew anything of my plans?'

Instinctively Liz raised her eyes to his. 'But you said....'

'I said that to make you fall in love with me seemed highly desirable,' Francisco corrected. 'And so it did!' He caressed her cheek softly with the back of his hand, winding a loose tendril of hair around one tanned finger. 'See how you hold me prisoner,' he said in husky tones, indicating his imprisoned hand.

'Francisco, you must explain to me!' Involuntarily Liz gripped his shoulder fiercely, willing him to put her out of her misery one way or another. She did not think that she could bear to have him build up her hopes and crush them.

'What do you think I mean, eh?'

'Please, Francisco!'

'Very well, *querida*. . . . My original intention, when issuing the invitation, was to prevent you from gaining a divorce. I am only human, and revenge seemed sweet after all that I had suffered since you left me.'

Liz ignored this statement for the moment and persisted: 'And then—what happened, Francisco?' In truth it was difficult to think at all, with his hard body pressed against her own, and the wild beating of his heart plainly demonstrating the disturbed state of his emotions.

'Then I met you again and realised that I had never stopped wanting you,' he said simply, his face stripped of its arrogance as he devoured her with his eyes. 'And now it is my turn to ask the questions, I think.' He placed a firm hand over her mouth, as she would have spoken. 'First things first, Lizbeth. Will you return to Spain with me, as my wife?' He raised her face gently to his own. 'Answer me, *querida*. I must know!'

Liz closed her eyes against the penetration in his own and shook her head wearily. 'You can take Edward to Spain, Francisco. I won't fight you! I must confess that I'd finally decided to run away with Edward, somewhere where you would never find us, but you needn't worry . . . I won't keep your son away from you any longer.'

'You mean that you will not come with me?' he said in anguished tones. 'Carlos said, and I also had begun to hope that you cared for me a little. Is it still Spencer that you love?' His voice broke on these words and he buried his face in the luxuriant softness of her hair.

'I have broken my engagement to John and I do care!

I do care for you, Francisco, but it's Edward you really want—I know that!'

'Of course I want my son, but not without you. If you cannot return my love, then you must keep Edward with you, here in England,' he said in calmer tones, moving his body gently away from her own. 'It would be cruel to deprive him of your presence.'

'Re—return your love?' she echoed.

'Is that not what I have said, Lizbeth? Do you want me to spell it out more clearly . . . do you want me to beg? If you do not return with me to Spain my life will be—empty.' He shrugged bleakly. 'But no doubt I will manage, as I have done for the last eight or nine years.'

With all her doubts removed, Liz leaned forward spontaneously and, holding Francisco's face between both her hands, placed her mouth softly over his own. For a moment she felt him stiffen beneath her embrace, then he was returning the pressure of her kiss, his lips forcing her own to open, devouring her mouth with his own.

'Not here, Lizbeth,' he groaned. 'Your bedroom. . . .'

'But. . . .'

'We are still married, are we not?' he said, with a trace of his old arrogance. 'You must learn to obey me . . . at least on these occasions,' he said huskily. 'I have no intention of letting you escape from me again!'

'You needn't worry, my darling,' Liz said softly, drawing him towards the stairs. 'I have no intention of going anywhere . . . except, of course, to bed,' she added provocatively.

A little more than six months later Liz was relaxing on a lounger beside the pool at Riera, her demure blue swimming costume not quite able to disguise the slightly swollen fullness of her healthily tanned body.

'Oh!' She jumped a little as a lithe, wet figure landed on the adjacent lounger.

'I am sorry, *querida*, I didn't mean to startle you,'

Francisco said in gentle tones.

'It wasn't your fault, darling. I'm afraid I was half asleep as usual, I don't seem to be able to keep my eyes open these days. You'd better put the blame on to the forthcoming addition to the Ramirez family,' she said with a smile.

Francisco stretched out a lazy hand and slowly traced the outlines of her swelling figure. 'I must confess that I find you infinitely desirable in your role as mother-to-be, Lizbeth. I believe I shall have to ensure that we have a very large family,' he said with a glint of laughter. 'Edward tells me that he is looking forward to having many brothers and sisters.'

'Men!' Liz exclaimed in mock exasperation. 'Am I not to have any say in the matter?'

'I think you may have to be consulted,' Francisco replied. Lines of laughter softened his normally austere features, causing Liz's heart to overflow with feeling as she looked at him.

'At least our large family won't have a jailbird for a father,' she said softly, leaning across the space between the loungers and drawing a caressing hand down the hard planes of his cheek.

'Did you really fear it, *querida*?' Francisco said with faint arrogance, drawing her hand to his mouth and kissing it softly. 'Diego never had any intention of continuing the legal action against me, he merely wished to cause me as much embarrassment as possible, but in reality he was the one to suffer the embarrassment.' He shrugged with contempt at the memory. 'His injuries were minor, but it was not possible for him to disguise the fact that he had been worsted in his encounter with me. He has had to endure a great deal of unpleasant gossip. In any event he was very well aware that his legal position was not a strong one. It was inevitable that he would withdraw the action,' Francisco finished dismissively.

'I was worried that it would prevent Marisa and Juan

from marrying ... or at least cause some friction between the families. I was very relieved when the wedding went off without a hitch,' Liz said reminiscently. 'And Juan's parents even seemed to have forgiven me for my behaviour at the dinner party.'

'I believe Juan told them about Luisa's attempts to disrupt our relationship ... that inevitably altered their preconceived notions a little. But I think they would find it harder to forgive if they knew that you were responsible for my sister's decision to continue her studies,' said Francisco, amusement evident in his voice.

'But I wasn't!' Liz protested explosively.

'I was only joking,' Francisco said with a laugh, holding up his arms to protect himself against imaginary blows.

'Seriously, Francisco, you didn't mind me encouraging Marisa to go to university, did you?' Liz sat up on the lounger, removing the dark glasses from her nose and regarding Francisco with a solemn expression. He reached out a hand and drew her face gently towards his own, placing a soft kiss on her warm mouth.

'Don't worry, Lizbeth, I was not angry. Have you perhaps failed to notice that you are able to wrap me around your little finger, hmm? Is that not the expression?'

'You ... you don't mind that I've kept in touch with John Spencer?' Liz asked softly, tracing the outline of his firmly shaped mouth with one tanned finger.

'I confess that I would prefer to keep you completely to myself,' he said in husky tones. 'I am a jealous man where you are concerned, my Lizbeth. But I do not forget that it was partly his honest assessment of your character and my behaviour towards you which helped to bring us together again, and Edward was very fond of Spencer. It would distress our son, I know, if he were to completely lose contact.'

'I don't think I could bear it if you wanted to keep in touch with Luisa Rodriguez,' Liz said softly. 'I sometimes feel that I'm not being fair to you ... the situation seems a little one-sided.'

'There is no comparison to be made between the two,' Francisco assured her, renewing his assault on her vulnerable mouth with mounting passion. 'It was sensible of her to go to stay with her sister in Madrid,' he said in hard tones. 'I have no wish to ever see Luisa Rodriguez again. We seem to be engaging in a great deal of serious conversation,' he said after a moment, removing the strap of her bodice with practised ease and exposing one perfect breast to his eager gaze, 'and I must confess that my thoughts lie in an altogether different direction.'

'Francisco,' Liz protested weakly. 'The servants. . . .'

'If I wish to make love to my wife in my own garden I will do so,' said Francisco with mock arrogance. 'However, as always, *querida*, your wish is my command,' and bending down he lifted her firmly into his arms and carried her towards the nearby summerhouse. 'I presume that you have no further objections to offer,' he said, kissing her softly and closing the door firmly behind them.

Harlequin® Plus
ROMANTIC SEVILLE

Imagine the sweet smell of orange blossoms floating on the air a warm spring evening. The streets are lined with sidewalk restaurants, filled with gaily dressed people chatting about the day's activities. Many enjoy a late dinner of succulent and spicy seafood in the open air, serenaded by the distant melodies of Gypsy violins. And afterward, perhaps a visit to a nearby club to see flamenco dancers.

This is the city of Seville, the most Spanish of Spanish cities; that reputation is well deserved, for to really get a "feel" for Spain, its people and its history, one need only experience Seville.

On the banks of the Guadalquivir River, only a few miles from the Atlantic Ocean, Seville was once a busy port for Greek and Phoenician sailors. It was later conquered by Julius Caesar, who made it the first Roman province; the Romans built villas, theaters and aqueducts. Later, Moroccan Moors built the fabulous Alcazar Palace with its lush gardens; a Moorish minaret, the Giralda, now forms the tower of the cathedral of Santa Maria, the third largest cathedral in Christendom. Such great explorers as Columbus, Cabot and Magellan sailed from Seville on their voyages of discovery. But that is history.

Today, Seville is a bustling trading center, famous for tobacco, ceramics, sherry, wine, olive oil, and oranges.

And romance. On those warm Sevillian nights there is always the enchantment of a stroll through the narrow winding streets of the medieval quarter, an embrace beside a fountain in a quiet courtyard, and the ever present perfume of orange blossoms.